Murder By Chocolate

A BITE-SIZED BAKERY COZY MYSTERY BOOK 1

ROSIE A. POINT

You're invited!

Hi there, reader!

I'd like to formally invite you to join my awesome community of readers. We love to chat about cozy mysteries, cooking, and pets.

It's super fun because I get to share chapters from yet-to-be-released books, fun recipes, pictures, and do giveaways with the people who enjoy my stories the most.

So whether you're a new reader or you've been enjoying my stories for a while, you can catch up with other like-minded readers, and get lots of cool content by visiting my website at *www.rosiepointbooks.com* and signing up for my mailing list.

Or simply search for me on *www.bookbub.com* and follow me there.

I look forward to getting to know you better.

Let's get into the story!

Yours,
Rosie

One

I SLIPPED OUT OF THE GUESTHOUSE IN THE DEAD of night. The salty smell of the ocean and the gentle wash of waves on the beach greeted me. The moon hung heavy and full in the inky black sky. A chilly breeze tugged at my thick woolen coat, cinched at the waist.

Spooky?

Not really.

Three a.m. was my favorite time of the night—it was ever so peaceful, and I got to spend the time I would've been tossing and turning in bed in my food truck instead.

Hey, that rhymes!

The adventure of being in a new town in Maine had my insomnia at an all-time high. How was a woman 'sposed to sleep with thoughts of lobster rolls and clam-bakes floating around?

I stopped in front of my food truck, a smile parting my lips. It was gorgeous, if I did say so myself. Candy-striped in pink-and-green pastels with a side window that opened out to serve the delicious baked goods we prepared fresh each day. Mostly Bee, my partner in baking, prepared them. I was still learning. But shoot, I was a good driver, at least.

The name "Bite-sized Bakery" was printed across the side of the truck in sweeping, curled letters. Pride swelled in my chest.

This was mine. All mine.

And I had this morning in Carmel Springs, right next to the beach, to admire it, get to work, and appreciate that I was finally done with the hurt hidden in my past.

"Have you heard about the ghost on Springs Wharf?" The voice floated out of the darkness behind me.

I let out a cry and threw up my arms. Unfortunately, I threw up the keys to my truck as well. They turned end-over-end once, then dropped on my head with a click. The merry jangle did nothing to help the sharp pain that came right after.

"Ow." The keys slid off my head and dropped on the sandy grass next to the truck. I bent and swept them up, straightened, and glared at the man who'd startled me. "Ow."

"Sorry about that," the guy said. "I didn't mean to scare ya."

"Maybe you shouldn't have crept up behind me then?"

The shock had finally started wearing off, and I took him in properly. He wore a fully waterproof suit—jacket and pants—and thick boots. His eyes were as blue as the ocean, his smile charming, and his hair dark and cut short.

Not bad at all. Not that I cared, of course. I'd already had one man disappear on me. I wasn't about to let another guy run off with my heart. Besides, I wouldn't be in Carmel Springs longer than three or four weeks. After Bee and I had served our food, we'd be off to the next small town.

That was our plan—explore the quaintest towns across the country. We'd meet the locals and experience the food while serving our delicious cakes, cookies, and donuts.

The guy whistled under his breath, and, for one horrible moment, I was sure he was catcalling me. But no, his gaze had switched to the truck. "That's a gorgeous piece of machinery you have there."

"Thanks," I said. "Look, I'm sorry, but can I help you with something? You stepped out of the dark talking about ghosts, and now you're..."

"Oh, shoot, ha. That's my bad. I got so caught up in, well, admiring you and your truck," he said and offered me another charming smile. "I was trying to figure out the best way to approach you."

"Why?"

I'd always been too inquisitive for my own good.

"Because you're pretty," he replied. "And because I was hoping this here truck was open. Wanted to grab myself something sweet before I headed out."

Is he... flirting with me? "Oh. Oh, well, we're not open yet," I said, awkwardly, trying to ignore the little voice in my head encouraging me to flirt back. "But, uh, I do have one of yesterday's chocolate mini-cakes in the fridge. I can't charge you for it, though. We only sell fresh."

"Really?"

"Yeah, sure. Why not?" I'd planned on eating it for my morning snack, but the guesthouse would have a full breakfast at nine. I was set on trying everything this small town had to offer regarding cuisine. "Hold on a second while I get it."

"Sure, that's great. I'm Owen, by the way. Owen Pelletier."

He stuck out a hand.

I chewed on the inside of my cheek. Ridiculous. It was a handshake, not a hug.

"Ruby Holmes."

"Pretty name to match your face."

Sheesh. At thirty-six years old, I'd left flirting in the past, along with my disappearing ex and my twenties.

"Wait right there," I said and hurried to the side door of my truck.

I unlocked it, the heels of my pumps clicking on the steps.

I returned with the boxed-up mini-cake.

"Here you go," I said.

"Thanks." Owen opened the pink-and-green striped box. "We don't get treats like this out on the water. I spotted your truck after we came in to the wharf yesterday evening. You were already closed, though."

"Yeah, we'd had a long day of traveling. But we'll be open all day today!"

My voice was unnaturally loud in the quiet. I searched around for something to say since Owen had repeatedly stared at me or the cake. "Um. You mentioned the wharf earlier. And a... ghost?"

Owen chuckled. "Ayuh. Rumor has it, there's a ghost of a woman who haunts the Springs Wharf. The legend says that she was the smitten lover of a fisherman who went out to sea and never came back. She spent every night waiting for him, but no news of what had happened ever came. She died of a broken heart, and now she walks the wharf, searching for him for all of eternity."

"Creepy."

I didn't like ghost stories. I preferred the real, the here, and the now.

"Really? I think it's sweet." He shrugged. "But I work that wharf every day, and I've never seen nothing."

"You're a fisherman?"

"Sternman on a lobster boat." His chest puffed out. "Shoot! Speaking of, I gotta get back before the captain tans my hide for being tardy." But Owen didn't immediately rush off. He scuffed the grass with the underside of his boot. "Say, you want to have dinner with me? I know places where the leaf peepers don't go."

"What's a leaf peeper?"

"Fall tourist."

"So me, basically," I said.

He laughed again. "Sure, but you're different. I can tell. What do you say? Meet me at the Lobster Shack at eight? You can bring a friend if you're scared."

It seemed like a challenge. And Owen didn't scare me anyway. I had mace in my purse and a black belt in karate because self-defense was a girl's best offense.

A date.

"Sure," I said. "Why not?"

There were a million reasons why not, but my mouth had betrayed me.

"Great!"

Then he was off, hurrying down the road and away to

the wharf—it was quite a way from the beach, past the pier, which was lit even now with quaint fairy lights and lampposts.

I let out a breath.

What a start to my first morning in Maine.

Then again, I'd hoped things would be exciting once Bee and I got on the road, and so far, it looked like this town would deliver.

Two

"HERE YOU GO," I SAID, HANDING THE BOXED-UP cake to the woman in front of the food truck's window.

The sun had already dipped below the horizon, marking the end of a productive and fun day baking, serving treats, and getting to know the locals in Carmel Springs. Most of them were friendly. Some of them were gruff. But all of them loved the food truck Bee and I had parked in front of the beach and close to our guesthouse.

"Have a lovely evening!" I called after the woman as she hurried off across the parking lot and to her car.

I took a second and inhaled the strange mix of our delicious baked treats and the salt coming off the sea. The ocean was timid this evening, the waves darting across the sand, touching and receding like a shy swimmer placing one toe into a cold pool.

"That's it," Bee said next to me. "I am officially pooped." My friend brushed her hands off on her pastel pink-and-green striped apron. "I think today has aged me about twenty years."

"So, you're finally looking your age, then?" I asked.

"Flattery will get you everywhere."

But it wasn't flattery. Bee was well into her sixties, but her spry attitude and her healthy habits had kept her slim, trim, and looking better than me, if I was honest. She wore her hair in a silver-white bob, and her smile, though slightly gap-toothed, always warmed my day.

It was strange, since we'd only been working together for a few weeks, but I felt closer to Bee than I had to most of my colleagues back at the *New York Tattler*.

After the "incident," I wanted nothing more than to get out of the big city and leave my investigative journalist job behind. And Bee, who was still somewhat of a mystery to me, had helped me do that—when I'd first put my ad in the paper for a baker on my food truck, one who'd be willing to travel across state lines and sleep in loads of motels and guesthouses, I'd expected no takers.

I'd been so convinced I'd considered retracting the ad and asking for my money back. After footing the bill for the food truck, ingredients, and the accessories needed for a successful business on the road, I'd been strapped for cash.

But then Bee had come knocking, and everything had changed.

I was eternally grateful to her for being willing to work with me, particularly since she was a fantastic baker.

I flashed an appreciative smile at her now.

"I take it you're smiling for a reason," Bee said as she wiped down the counters in our truck with a rag. "Why don't you tell me more about this date you've got tonight?"

My stomach did a little flip. I'd forgotten about Owen, the handsome and surprising lobsterman who'd asked me out. I checked my filigree watch, its pearlescent face flashing the time.

It was already 7:30 pm. I had to be at the Lobster Shack in half an hour.

"Oh my heavens, I'm going to be late."

"Late? Late for a very important date?" Bee grinned at me.

I flapped my hands at her. "I wouldn't say it's important. I have no idea why I even agreed to go on a date with him. It was all so strange."

I broke down what had happened this morning for her —Bee had rolled out of bed an hour after the incident and had been too grumpy to ask too many questions at the time.

"He scared you?" Bee asked. "That's an interesting way to ask someone out on a date."

"I shouldn't even be going. Not after..."

Bee blinked at me. I hadn't yet told her my full story, and she never pressured me into it. I liked that about her. She respected my privacy, and I did the same for her, though I *was* curious about her history. She had shared even less than I had.

Not that it mattered—we shared a love for baking and were both loyal and trustworthy. Bee had a fantastic sense of humor too, which always helped during the long hours on the truck.

I cleared my throat. "Look, I'll tell you later, but now, I've got to get changed and get to this Lobster Shack place."

"Knock on my door when you're back at the guesthouse, all right? Just so I know you haven't gotten lost between here and the pier."

"And because you'd like to know what happened?"

"That too."

I paused, looking around the truck. Not everything was neatly polished and packed away for tomorrow. "The truck..."

"I'll handle this." Bee flicked my arm with her rag. "Go on. You go have some fun."

I hastily untied my apron, left it on one of the hooks

next to the specials board, and hurried out into the night. A quick trip to the guesthouse for a freshening-up later, and I was on my way to the pier—I'd looked up the address of the Lobster Shack earlier—my heart hammering in my chest.

My palms had grown sweaty.

This so wasn't like me. Maybe it was good I got out of my comfort zone and forgot about Daniel. After all, it *had* been two years. Two whole years of my colleagues giving me the side-eye and muttering things behind my back, and I'd probably imagined most of it, but I certainly hadn't imagined the pain of losing him.

Now really isn't the time to be thinking about that.

I found the pier still bustling with activity, folks meandering along its wooden walkway and stopping to play games at stalls or to shop for touristy items to take home from their trip to the seaside town.

The Lobster Shack was supposed to be right at the end of the pier. The closer I got to the restaurant, the quieter the pier grew. Odd. The other portions of the pier had been so busy and full of life—surely, a popular seafood restaurant would draw in a lot of tourists and locals?

I arrived at the restaurant and found it in darkness. The front doors were glass and huge, looking out on the ocean, along with several floor-to-ceiling windows. I spied a bar further back, but no activity whatsoever.

The hairs on the back of my neck stood on end, and I reached into my purse for my mace. I took a step toward the restaurant, craning my neck, but stopped in my tracks. The front door was ajar.

"Hello?" I called out. "Is anyone in there? Owen?"

I wasn't about to waltz into a restaurant so clearly devoid of life. But my curiosity was piqued for the second time that day. Why would the lobsterman have invited me to a closed restaurant?

I positioned myself in front of the door and opened it slowly. The light from the lampposts on the pier splashed across the wooden boards.

I didn't have to take a step inside to make out the shape on the floor.

A man, lying supine, a smear of something dark across his cheek. A lobster mallet lay a few feet from him, its end coated in something red. Something I was sure was blood.

It was my date, Owen.

And he was dead.

Three

"AND YOU JUST HAPPENED TO BE HERE TO FIND the body?"

The detective, a squat little man who wore a scowl that transformed him into a caricature of a villain, sat with his notepad and pen on his lap and glared at me.

"I didn't just happen to be here," I said, shifting on the bench at the end of the pier. "I was here for a date."

"With the deceased."

"Yes."

I'd already told him that about five times, but Detective Jones, the incarnation of every small town mean police officer cliché, hadn't taken any of it in. That, or he just wanted to question me until we were both blue in the face.

And given that it was fall, and the chilly wind off the

ocean had dropped a few degrees in the past half an hour, we'd likely change color or freeze at this rate.

I shifted on the bench, my gaze darting toward the restaurant and away again. Each time I looked over at it— now with crime scene tape out front and police officers moving around the entrance, talking softly—my stomach did a turn, flip, and a plunge.

Owen was dead.

I had never seen a dead body before. No, that wasn't right. I'd never seen a *murdered* body. The only time I'd experienced anything similar had been at my Great Aunt Tiana's funeral, where there'd been an open casket. I'd been fifteen years old at the time and passed out right in front of the coffin. Twenty years had passed, but I wasn't any less squeamish.

It was much easier to write articles about war, famine, or death than to confront them face-to-face.

I squeezed my eyes shut and caught my breath.

"Tell me what you saw again," Detective Jones said in that commanding tone.

I faced him. "I didn't see anything except... except poor Owen on the floor. He had a smudge of something on his cheek, and there was a lobster mallet next to him. I—I didn't see anything else. Or anyone else."

"A lobster mallet," Jones said. "Interesting that you remember that detail."

"It was fairly obvious, given that it was covered in blood." I shuddered. "Look, what's your point?"

Detective Jones took his time writing something down on his notepad, underlining it three times, viciously.

"Detective, may I go? I've given you my statement and answered all your questions. I don't see how—"

"You know when we last had a murder in Carmel Springs?" he asked.

"No. I'm new to town."

"That's what I thought." He snapped his notepad closed. "The last time we had a murder was last fall during tourist season. All these leaf peepers come down here, thinking they belong. They bring trouble with them. The guy whodunit the last time? He was a tourist, too."

"Too?" I stiffened. "What on earth are you suggesting?"

"That you don't leave town," he replied. "Not until this investigation is over."

I hadn't planned on leaving for another few weeks, but the fact that I couldn't now sat in the back of my mind. What if the customers here didn't buy? What if we needed to move on? Just how long did a murder investigation usually take to—

"Ruby!" A shout traveled along the pier.

Both the crotchety detective and I looked up.

Bee came scuttling toward me, still wearing her Bite-sized Bakery apron from the truck.

"I heard the sirens," she said. "And then some old guy came by and told me that there'd been a murder at the restaurant."

"Which old guy?" Detective Jones and I asked in unison.

We exchanged a glance, one that was fraught with dislike and tension.

"You let me handle the questions, young lady," he said.

He was probably five years older than me and a few inches shorter. Not that there was anything wrong with short, but still... "young lady?"

"Who are you?" Bee asked, eying the detective. "A rent-a-cop?"

"No, Bee, he's a real detective. Investigating the case."

Jones had drawn himself up straight at the phrase "rent-a-cop."

"Who died?" Bee asked, looking over her shoulder at the restaurant.

"I'll fill you in later," I said. "Detective, are we done here? Am I allowed to leave?"

"No," Jones said, his beady brown eyes narrowing. "I still have a few questions about your involvement."

"What involvement?" Bee asked.

"Ma'am, I'm going to need you to back up. This is an

ongoing police investigation, and I need to question Miss Holmes as a person of interest in the case."

Bee pursed her lips at the detective but retreated after a few moments, hanging back near the railing at the touristy stall closest to the restaurant. She peered out over the ocean but cast surreptitious looks our way as if checking whether I needed her help.

I took a deep breath and focused. "Wait, I'm a person of interest?"

This can't be happening.

He couldn't seriously think I had anything to do with this. But then, his whole leaf peeper speech had pretty much insinuated that.

"Look," I said. "I didn't do anything wrong. Owen asked me out on a date this morning. All I did was turn up here at the right time and—"

"You expect me to believe that he invited you to have dinner at a restaurant that's always closed on a Monday?"

"I didn't know that. I was asked out on a date. I spent all day working. I didn't even have time to—"

"Why would he ask you to this place if it was closed?"

"I have no idea," I said. "I wasn't the one doing the asking." Prickles danced over my skin—this always happened when I got frustrated. First came the prickles, and then I'd get hot, and then I'd say something I'd regret. "This is ridiculous. I've cooperated with you fully, and I've done absolutely nothing wrong except get the shock of my life." I swallowed, trying to calm myself down. "Look, I'm staying at the Oceanside Guesthouse. If you need to talk to me again, I'll be there. And I'm going to park my food truck down at the beach every day too."

Detective Jones tapped his pen on his pad one last time. "Fine," he said at last. "You can go. But I'll be in touch, Miss Holmes. Don't go anywhere."

"I wasn't planning on it."

I rose from the bench.

I wobbled slightly and steadied myself on the wrought-iron arm. It was the murder. It had me woozy. That or the detective's line of questioning had sent me into a dizzy state. Either way, I had to get off this pier.

I met Bee in front of the stall, and she looped an arm around my shoulders.

"Are you all right? You look like you've seen, well, exactly what you just saw."

"A corpse," I said.

"Now, there's something that will keep you up all night."

"I hope not. We're supposed to open the truck early tomorrow."

But Bee was right. If I closed my eyes now, I'd wind up running the whole event through my head again.

"Come on," my friend said. "Let's get you back to the

guesthouse. We can have some hot cocoa before bed and talk about what happened."

"Do you really think talking will help?"

"It's better than lying awake, staring at the ceiling."

Bee patted me on the back.

I cast a last glance at the Lobster Shack. Detective Jones was out front and stared at me as we walked away, his mouth set in a thin line.

Four

THE GUESTROOMS WE'D HIRED OUT IN THE Oceanside Guesthouse were small but quaint and linked through a shared bathroom. We'd opted to leave the doors open for now, which I greatly preferred since I was spooked out after the whole "dead body in the restaurant" incident.

I sat on the armchair at the end of Bee's bed in her suite and curled my legs underneath myself. The guesthouse was mostly self-service, with set meals for dinner, breakfast, and lunch if one booked to eat.

Unfortunately, it was way too late for us to attend the dinner, and the guesthouse didn't have room service. However, there was a station for coffee, hot cocoa, and tea in the corner of every room, and it was there that Bee stood now, humming under her breath as she fixed us two mugs of hot cocoa and plopped mini-marshmallows into the frothy chocolatey liquid.

She brought the mugs over to the tiny seating area and handed one to me before settling into her armchair and propping her feet up on the coffee table.

"I've got an ache in my toes," she said. "And in my neck. And one in my brain from all the customers this morning."

Bee was friendly to me, but she was definitely a behind-the-scenes type of person. She preferred baking to talking to folks, whereas I enjoyed discovering the strange personalities in this small town.

"The toes and the neck might need a soak in the tub," I said. "I'm afraid I don't know what to do about the brain pain."

"I'm thinking a good set of earplugs might do the trick," she replied, smiling. But her mirth faded. "How are you? You were so pale when I arrived on the pier. You looked like a ghost."

"I know I need a tan," I said, tugging my warm fluffy robe toward my body, "but that's a bit harsh."

Bee chuckled.

I took a sip of my hot cocoa to bolster myself and nearly burned my top lip on a marshmallow. I scooped it out with a greedy finger and deposited it into my mouth, relishing the sweetness as it spread over my tongue and warmed me.

The sugar helped, that was for sure. I no longer felt as if I was about to keel over or faint, or worse.

"All right, so what do you think happened?" Bee set her mug down on her lap, grasping it between her palms.

"I know what happened," I said. "Someone murdered Owen with a lobster mallet."

Bee, who had lifted her mug to take another sip of cocoa, snorted and nearly did a spit take. "I'm sorry, what?"

"A lobster mallet."

"As in the tool? The tool used to crack open the lobster shell and get to the succulent meat inside?"

"I wasn't aware there was another kind of lobster mallet," I replied.

"No, no, there isn't. I think. I just wanted to be sure we're on the same page," she replied. "A lobster mallet. Now, that *is* unique. What kind of murderer walks around with a lobster mallet?"

"I have no idea," I said, and I didn't shudder this time. It was much easier to discuss this when I wasn't in the shadow of a murder scene.

"Perhaps a roving diner, angry about the fact that they hadn't yet sated their hunger?"

"Bee..."

"I know, I know, not an appropriate joke, but still. It's a strange weapon choice," she said. "As murder weapons go, I don't think I've ever heard of a lobster mallet killing."

"Haven't spent much time in Florida?"

"I thought that was the chainsaw massacre state? Or was it shotguns? Shovels?"

"Are you trying to make me dizzy?" I asked. "You know how I am with blood. And I just saw a whole mallet coated in the stuff."

"Yuck. Sorry. And I'm sorry about your date too. This Owen guy sounded nice. Albeit strange."

I took another sip of cocoa, thinking about my brief acquaintance with poor Owen. "I wonder who did it?"

Bee met my gaze and held it for a moment. "Me too."

I didn't know what Bee had done in her past. Her resume had been sparse, apart from a yearlong stint at a patisserie in Soho and a certificate proving that she'd taken a two-year baking course. Before that, there was nothing. I hadn't asked, even though I'd been sufficiently curious to do a quick online search that hadn't turned up much.

But I trusted her implicitly. Bee was one of those people who had an open smile and said exactly what they meant. I liked that, particularly since I'd spent so much time interviewing people for articles on topics they didn't want to talk about.

"You know," Bee said, scooping one of her marshmallows out of her cocoa and slurping it down, "motive is important. And the question is valid. Who would be walking around with a lobster mallet? Was running into Owen accidental or intentional? And how on earth did they know he would be in that restaurant?"

"Well, the place was called the Lobster Shack. Maybe the killer grabbed the mallet from the kitchen or the bar or something?"

"Maybe."

"An even better question would be why on earth Owen asked me to go out to eat at a restaurant that was known for being closed on Monday evenings? It doesn't make sense."

"Hmm. That is strange."

Bee sank into a quiet.

It was broken by the gentle creak of the bathroom door.

Bee and I tensed immediately. I set my cocoa down, trembling, and peered at the darkened crack between the edge of the bathroom door and the jamb.

"Who's there?" I called out.

Bee rose from her chair. "Come out, right now," she said. "We know you're in there."

The door creaked again, and my heart pitter-pattered like crazy.

A calico cat paw reached around the bottom of the

door and hooked claws into the wood. Another creak, and a kitty cat leaped into view with a meow and a purr.

Bee burst out laughing. "It's a cat. Of course, it's a cat."

For a moment, I'd thought a lobster-mallet-wielding psychopath had been hiding in the bathroom. I giggled, and the kitty cat meowed and darted over to me. It rubbed its cute face against my legs, purring loudly.

"Who are you?" I asked, and scratched behind its ears.

"I think that's Samantha's cat," Bee said. "She mentioned it this morning at breakfast. It's a tom."

The cat's collar jingled, and I caught the name tag between my fingers. "Trouble," I said. "His name is Trouble."

"Fitting, given that he nearly scared the cocoa out of my hands."

I grinned and kept on stroking Trouble. "I've always wanted a cat."

"Why didn't you ever get one?"

I paused, thinking over how to word the answer. "Well, I've never had the chance. My ex was allergic, and now that we're on the road..."

Bee nodded. "Seems like you'll have Trouble's company while we're in Carmel Springs." She paused, then broke out in peals of laughter. "I just realized how that sounds."

"You're not wrong. Trouble has certainly found me."

Hopefully, the only type that would accompany me through my day tomorrow would be the furry, purring kind.

Five

I STIFLED A YAWN AS I TOOK ANOTHER ORDER FOR a mudslide chocolate cake and handed out change. I hadn't gotten a wink of sleep after the whole "lobster mallet murder" thing, and Trouble had spent the night on the end of my bed, purring and massaging my comforter.

"Careful," Bee said as I yawned a second time. "Keep doing that, and you'll swallow someone whole."

I managed a watery-eyed smile as I dished a delectable mudslide chocolate mini-cake into one of our branded boxes. Bee was a master at making these. They were ever so chocolatey, with a fudge frosting on the outside, a moist cake beneath it, and a runny, oozy chocolate-filled center.

"These are delicious," the customer said as she accepted the box. "I had one yesterday morning."

I vaguely remembered her from my early morning stint in the truck. She'd definitely introduced herself to me, and though I usually had a knack for placing names with faces, I pulled a blank now.

The woman, blonde, slim, petite, and in her twenties, from what I could tell, offered me a smile. "It's Grace," she said. "Grace Allen. We met yesterday morning?"

"I remember. Sorry, I'm exhausted and forgetful this morning. How are you, Grace?"

"Oh, doing fine. Just fine. Well, fine, given the circumstances." She rounded her words nicely. "You heard about what happened at the Lobster Shack?"

"Yes. Regrettably," I said.

Bee took over the register, and I stepped to one side in the truck, Grace following me to continue the conversation.

It was always good to get to know the locals, and I had come to soak up the atmosphere in the small town. Granted, I hadn't planned on soaking up a murder while I was at it.

"Terrible way to go," Grace said softly, her fingers clutching the cake box.

"Terrible," I agreed. "I suppose folks around here are shaken up about it."

Grace shrugged. "I guess."

"No?"

"Some of them are," she said. "But most are carrying on. It's the New England way. That and... no, I shouldn't say."

"Please do," I replied. "This gossip session is helping to wake me right up."

Grace's lips, crimson with lipstick, parted. "Between you and me, Owen wasn't exactly the most popular guy around here. You know, he got under a lot of people's skin. I should know. I work at the Lobster Shack. He was always around. And he—"

The whoop of a police siren cut across Grace's words.

The car had parked right next to the truck. The long line of customers turned their heads as Detective Jones emerged from the cruiser.

"Uh oh," Bee muttered. "Looks like Danny DeVito is back to question us again."

"Bee."

"You're right, Danny DeVito is a talented man. A treasure." Bee nodded to the detective. "Can't say the same for him."

"Bee."

"Don't expect me to be civil," she hissed. "Terrible excuse for an officer. The way he treated you last night..."

Grace had already backed away from the window, and the other customers did the same, making way for the detective as he strode importantly through the crowd, casting glances left and right and readjusting his belt.

"All right," Jones called out. "Everyone back up. Back away from the food truck."

"Excuse me," I said. "What do you think you're doing?"

"You can't chase our customers away," Bee put in.

I exited the truck, clattered down the side steps, and came face-to-face with the detective. The fall morning was chilly, but Jones wore a thin veneer of sweat on his ruddy cheeks.

"You can't chase off—"

"Everyone clear out. This truck is being confiscated," Detective Jones said, "by order of a judge." He flashed a piece of paper at me, and I grabbed it, scanning the document.

"Let me see that." Bee trundled down the stairs behind me. She held the paper close to her nose since she didn't have her reading glasses and frowned. "Shoot. It's a warrant."

"A warrant?" I said it too loudly, and a murmur spread through the crowd of onlookers.

Over near the benches that looked out on the beach, Grace set down the box of cake she'd just paid for and backed away from it.

"Why? Why are you doing this?" I asked.

The eager listeners hadn't left, and Detective Jones scowled at the question. "Come with me, ma'am."

We walked around to the back of the truck, out of earshot of the onlookers and listeners. Bee came too, marching instead of walking and glaring at the back of the detective's head.

Detective Jones turned on us. "I'm confiscating this truck because it is now an active part of a murder investigation."

"What?"

"That's impossible," Bee said. "The truck was nowhere near the pier yesterday."

"Owen Pelletier wasn't just hit over the head. Preliminary reports indicate that he was poisoned as well, and since the last thing Owen was seen eating was a slice of your cake..."

My eyes widened. "That's not... No. You can't do this. There's no poison on my truck, and there's no way he died because of one of our cakes."

"If that's true," Jones said, and his lips curled downward at the corners, "you won't have anything to worry about. You'll have your truck back before the end of the week. But for now, it's being confiscated. An officer will escort you into the truck to remove any personal effects you might have left inside. After that, you're done."

"But there's a tray of mudslide minis in the oven," I said.

Bee's hand settled on my forearm. "I don't think they care about the minis, Ruby."

We were guided back into the truck by another younger and less mean officer and allowed to collect our handbags and phones. Detective Jones grabbed the keys to the truck himself, all while our would-be customers looked on.

Shame curled through my belly. This was exactly what I hadn't wanted when I'd decided to go on this trip—too much negative attention. It was why I'd chosen a food truck, not a restaurant. We could easily move on from one town to the next, and I would *never* have to settle down in a place where embarrassment could catch up with me.

But now, the food truck was gone, and our only escape was too.

Bee and I stood side-by-side as the truck was taken away.

"What now?" Bee asked.

I hesitated, chewing on the inside of my cheek. "We get the truck back."

"But how, Ruby? I get the feeling that the 'good' detective won't be giving it up any time soon."

"We figure out who killed Owen."

I set my jaw.

I'd investigated plenty of strange cases during my stint as a journalist. This would be no different. Apart from the fact that it would probably be a little more dangerous. Okay, a lot more. But still.

"I'm with you," Bee said.

We turned and headed off down the street, back toward the Oceanside Guesthouse.

Six

"ARE YOU SURE YOU'LL BE FINE?" BEE ASKED AS
she checked her reflection in the bathroom mirror.

She had chosen a red trench coat cinched at the waist,
paired with jeans and a blouse beneath it.

I had selected a woolen dress, thick leggings, and a pair
of ankle-high boots that clicked when I walked. The sound
was pleasant, and I fixated on that instead of worrying
about the evening ahead. The news of what had happened
that afternoon had likely traveled.

I'd grown up in a small town and understood exactly
how they worked. People were always in everyone else's
business, sometimes in a harmless way or out of concern,
but I couldn't, by any stretch of the imagination, assume
that the folks of Carmel Springs would be concerned
for me.

I was new. And one of the locals was dead.

"Ruby?"

I tucked my chestnut brown hair behind my ears, enjoying that it was short now. *Daniel never wanted me to cut it.* "Sorry, Bee, my mind is all over the place."

"That's why I'm asking," she said. "Are you sure you want to go back to that restaurant?"

"Of course," I replied. "We made a booking, and it *is* the scene of the crime. I'm surprised they opened it up so soon after what happened."

"It doesn't take too long to search a scene for evidence if the forensic team is on point," Bee replied, sweeping mascara over her lashes.

I frowned. "How do you know?"

Bee capped the mascara and gave me the side-eye. "I watch a lot of crime scene investigation shows." And then she skedaddled out of our bathroom to collect her purse.

I didn't quite buy her excuse, but I wasn't about to pry, just like she wouldn't poke into my personal business or ask me strange questions about the things I did or didn't know. It was nice to have a friend who cared enough not to put me in an awkward position. That was easy and fun rather than pressured and full-on.

I collected my handbag from the end of my bed and gave Trouble a scratch behind the ears—he'd hung around me all afternoon, even while we'd had tea and cookies in the guesthouse's living room.

Finally, we were out the door and walking along the road that led past the beach and toward the pier. The wharf was further down, occupied by fishing boats. Had Owen eaten my mini-cake out there?

We made our way onto the pier and past locals and tourists. It was clear who was who there. Most of the locals stared and whispered when they caught sight of us.

"...from the food truck."

"...Poison?"

"...should just leave. Outsiders."

I chewed on the inside of my cheek, and Bee patted me on the back. "Don't let them get to you. Not everyone will have that opinion of us. Innocent until proven guilty," she said the last part loudly.

Perhaps it was my imagination, or that I was jumpy after the murder and Detective Jones' confiscation of the truck, but it sure felt as if the gazes followed us all the way to the Lobster Shack.

The front doors were open, and laughter and music drifted out along with the smells of cooking—fish and fries and chowders, garlic, and butter, and oh my.

My mouth watered.

A waiter stepped out from behind a wooden podium

and offered us both a smile. "Hi there. Welcome to the Lobster Shack. How may I help you?"

"We have a booking under the name Holmes," I replied. "For two?"

"Of course." The waiter checked a list of names and grabbed two menus from a dispenser attached to the stand. "Right this way. I've got you seated out on the deck."

His friendly attitude helped me relax. Bee was right: not everyone would instantly hate us. And we hadn't done anything wrong.

We exited onto the deck and sat at one of the tables with a gorgeous ocean view. The moon had only just arced into the sky, casting its glow on the waters below. A fire roared in a central iron-grated pit, shedding its warmth underneath the overhang.

The waiter lit a lamp on our table and then handed us the menus.

"Thank you." I opened mine and browsed.

Bee scanned the outside of the restaurant, occasionally wriggling her nose or narrowing her eyes.

"That's strange," I said, paging through the menu.

"What is?"

"The lobster dishes on the menu have been scratched out. Is it the same in your menu?"

Bee opened hers and paged, turning the thick card between her fingers. "Yes, it's the same."

"Good evening!" The merry tone came from our waitress.

"Grace," I said.

It was the same woman who'd ordered the mini-cake from us this morning before the detective had confiscated the truck.

"You're our server?"

"Yes," Grace said, smiling as she brought a notepad out of the front pouch of her apron.

"Sorry, our conversation got interrupted this morning."

This was our opportunity. She had been in the middle of telling me about Owen—how he hadn't exactly been the most popular guy around. What if she knew more? Maybe she could tell us who'd been enemies with Owen.

"Oh, that's okay. Sorry your truck got taken away. Between you and me, I think that Jones doesn't know what he's doing," Grace said, lowering her voice to a conspiratorial whisper. "Owen was hated by just about everyone."

"Everyone?" I asked.

"Well, yeah. Especially the waitresses here. He used to flirt with them." She pressed her lips together and shifted her eyes left and right, checking that none of the other waitstaff or customers could hear us. "And he did more than just that."

"Like what?" Bee asked.

"He got into a fight with the chef," she said. "I'm not sure why, though." Another waiter exited onto the deck, and Grace straightened, hastily neatening her apron. "Anyway. Um, can I get you something to drink or eat?"

"Sure," I said. "I'll have a banana milkshake, please."

"Strawberry for me," Bee said, then pointed to the menu and its scratched out items. "You don't have lobster rolls?"

Grace shook her head. "We've had a problem with our supplier, so all our lobster menu items aren't available at the moment. Sorry."

"Oh. Oh, all right. Then I'll guess I'll have the cheesy garlic bread and the fried Maine oysters," I said, my mouth already watering.

My brain definitely had food for thought, too—Owen had argued with the chef. Why? And about what?

"And I'll have the New England salt of the seafood chowder, please."

Bee handed the menu over, and Grace hurried off into the restaurant.

"That was interesting," I said, after she was gone. "What do you think? Should we talk to the chef after our meal?"

"That sounds like a good idea to me. Suppose this Owen guy was so hated by everyone. In that case, it stands to reason that someone around here would have had the motive to murder him," Bee whispered back, her hazel eyes alive with excitement. "Let's hang around for a while. Have some dessert too."

A night away from the guesthouse would be fun, and if we managed to find out more about what had happened to Owen... well, even better.

The sooner I got the food truck back, the happier I'd be—it was my dream, and it had been snatched away by a detective who clearly didn't like me one bit.

Seven

THE LAUGHTER IN THE RESTAURANT HAD DIED down quite some time ago, and fall's cold bite had grown stronger as the evening had worn on, well into the night. The moon was full and round and absolutely beautiful over the water, but, for once, I was kind of spooked out.

The quieter it got, the more my thoughts turned toward what had happened to Owen. And right there, in the restaurant, we'd enjoyed a meal, dessert, milkshakes, sodas, and then another entrée because why not?

We weren't technically on holiday, but it sure felt like it. The last time I'd sat and enjoyed the view, even if it was chilly underneath the overhang attached to the restaurant's side, had been, shoot, I couldn't remember.

"The fire's dying down," Bee said, gesturing to the pit.

She shivered and rubbed the arms of her coat. "And it looks like the staff are getting ready to clean up."

"That's our cue." I raised my hand and scribbled in mid-air.

A few moments later, Grace hurried out with the check and handed it over. I took some money out and placed it on the little saucer that held the receipt. "Thank you so much, Grace," I said. "This was lovely."

"Lovely," Bee echoed.

Grace bobbed her head, smiling. "I'm glad you enjoyed it. The restaurant's been quieter lately, you know with the whole lobster problem. And the murder."

"That tends to dissuade people," Bee said. "Corpses aren't exactly the fine-dining esthetic most folks are looking for."

Grace didn't seem to know how to respond to that. Bee did have a strange sense of humor, one I happened to like.

"Grace," I said, directing her back to me. "Could we talk to the chef? You know, the food was so delicious. It would be great to compliment him on it in person."

"Oh, sure." She hurried off to fetch him.

"What a strange woman," Bee said.

"Strange? Why?"

"Oh, I don't know, maybe it's just me that's strange.

I'm not the type who'll share everything so openly, and she was more than happy to gossip."

"You've never lived in a small town before, have you?"

Bee laughed. "Maybe that's it."

We waited a few moments, chewing on some mints Grace had brought to our table until a figure in chef's whites finally appeared. He trudged out of the back door and toward us. His coat was surprisingly clean—if it was me in there, I'd have probably burnt my shirt sleeves—and he was young too.

And handsome. Not that it was appropriate to think that about a suspect. *A suspect? What are you, a police officer?*

"You called?" The chef winked at me, and my heart did a little sputter-flip.

What on earth was wrong with me? This was the second man who'd flirted in the last two days, and given what had happened to the first...

"Hello," I said.

"And hello," Bee put in. "I'm the blurry object in your peripheral vision." She waved.

I had to press my hand over my mouth to keep from laughing.

"Hi," the chef said, winking at her too.

"Shameless." Bee returned a cheeky wink. "I like that in a chef."

"What about in a man?"

"Hmmm," Bee said. "You'll have to ask my ex-husband about that. If you can find him. He went missing, you know, off the coast of Costa Rica. After a long vacation with his mistress. I've always wondered what happened to him."

That drained the color from the chef's face.

I laughed out loud this time. I wasn't sure if Bee was serious—though my insides had twisted when she'd said "missing"—but the chef's reaction was priceless.

"I'm kidding, of course." Bee grinned. "Or am I?"

"We called you out here because we wanted to meet the person who made us such a delicious meal."

"Oh." That brightened the chef's mood. He wore his dark hair short and neat, and he was exceptionally tall. Strong too, if his wide-set shoulders were any indication. "Well, that would be me."

"Really? It wasn't another winking man in an identical outfit?"

I nudged Bee under the table with the toe of my boot, and she grinned and raised her hands. "Fine, fine, I'll leave him alone."

"Bee's got quite the sense of humor," I said, smiling up at the chef. "I'm Ruby, by the way."

"Miller," he said. "First name. I know it's strange, but

that's what my parents chose to call me. No use being mad about it."

"It could be worse." Bee shifted to the edge of her seat, trying to get closer to the fire. "You could be named Sue."

"Sue?"

"It's a song. Johnny Cash. Oh, the youth of today," Bee said. "Would you like to sit down, Chef Miller? I'm going to get closer to the fire, and I have the feeling that you and Ruby will have a lot to talk about."

She got up before I could protest or the chef could reply.

Miller sat down in the spot she'd vacated and placed his hands atop the table. "Weird lady," he said.

"Nice," I corrected. "And it's also nice to meet you, Miller. The food you prepared tonight was delicious." Now, to broach the topic of the murder. And the rumor of his disagreement with the victim. I was used to prying information out of people, thankfully. One couldn't be a journalist without having the knack for a little manipulation. Not my finest quality, but it would help here.

"It's what I love to do."

"Even during such difficult times," I said. "I admire that."

"Difficult times?" Miller scratched his forehead. "Oh right, yeah. The murder."

"The murder." I pulled a face. "Terrible thing to happen. And what a way to go. A lobster mallet."

"Poisoning's what I heard." Miller shrugged, as if he didn't much care which way it had happened. "Wasn't like the guy was well-liked around here. Or anywhere in town."

"He wasn't?" It would probably be a bad idea to ask Miller directly about him fighting with the victim. But I could press for information, nonetheless.

"Naw. Owen had a knack for rubbing folks the wrong way. And for landing himself in trouble."

Apparently, Owen and I shared that particular proclivity.

"Oh. Well, what do you mean by that? There are all types of trouble. Most types shouldn't lead to murder."

"Right." Miller shrugged a second time, the stiff starch in his shirt bringing a scrape of fabric as he moved. "What can I say? Guy was a lowlife. He's part of the reason the restaurant's been struggling like it has."

"How so?" I'd gotten Miller exactly where I wanted him—my comfort zone. With him talking. Telling me, naturally, all the things he probably wouldn't tell a stranger. I might've been squeamish about blood and bodies and the whole lobster mallet fiasco, but this was easy. This was fun.

"I shouldn't say." Miller glanced back at Bee, who was

out of earshot, standing by the dying embers in the grate, her palms out. "But, oh well, it won't hurt, will it? Anyway, Owen works for the guy who supplies the lobster to most of the restaurants in town. Basically, he runs the wharf, right, so he chooses exactly who goes out on which boat and who the lobsters are sold to."

"Oh?" I frowned.

"That guy, Mr. Dillington? Rumor has it that he won't sell any lobster to the guy who owns the restaurant because he's taken a particular dislike to Owen. And it's Owen's uncle, Benjamin, who runs the Lobster Shack."

"Wait, so Mr. Dillington won't supply Benjamin with lobster because he doesn't like Owen?"

"Sounds crazy, don't it?"

"Yes."

It sounded unbelievable. I didn't know much about lobster fishing, but as I understood it, the guy who owned the dock would buy from the fishing boats and then sell to suppliers. Was Mr. Dillington not buying fish from Owen's boat? Or did Dillington captain the boat himself? Perhaps he didn't allow other businesses to fish at the dock?

"It's what I overheard. Benjamin argued with Owen because Owen had messed up so badly at work that he'd compromised everything for the restaurant. Folks run in circles around here. You scratch my back, and I scratch yours, see? So Benjamin gets Owen the job down at the wharf as a sternman on one of the boats, and then Owen steals lobster, and there you have it. No more lobster for the Shack."

"But if Owen had stolen lobster, surely his boss would have fired him?" I asked.

The chef shrugged his broad shoulders. "Maybe they couldn't prove it."

"Maybe."

It was confusing, but it had definitely given me my next lead. I needed to talk to this boss of Owen's at the wharf. He'd likely have more information about Owen's last days, and if there was a feud ongoing, then either the boss or even Owen's uncle might have had reason to take matters into their own hands.

There were a few missing links, but I got the feeling that I was closer to solving the mystery.

"You're pretty."

The compliment had come out of left field.

The chef wore a goofy grin and winked at me again. "Would you like to come to dinner with me some time?"

I'd learned my lesson about this already. First, I'd been bitten by my fiancé leaving me in the lurch, and then I'd almost gone on a date with a man who'd wound up dead. "I think I'm all done with dating," I said. "The last time didn't work out so well. But thanks for the offer. And for talking to me."

Bee and I headed out of the restaurant and back home, our bellies full and our minds questioning. What would tomorrow bring?

And who exactly had killed Owen Pelletier?

Eight

I HAD NEVER HAD A LOT OF FREE TIME. NOT WHEN I had been engaged to Daniel, who'd always had a busy schedule as a business owner, or when I'd worked as a journalist. And now, the food truck was gone, and I was left feeling empty.

At least, that was how I would have felt if not for Bee.

She hummed as she fixed us a pot of coffee in the corner of my room, setting out the mugs and insisting that I have a little sugar to sweeten my morning.

"Today is going to be a big day," Bee said. "You'll need your strength."

"I'm sure sugar won't provide me with strength."

"But it might make you hyperactive. And we'll need all the energy, vim, and vigor we can get if we run into that shriveled walnut of a human being again."

"You're referring to Detective Jones?" I asked, hiccupping a laugh.

"The very same." Bee brought a mug over to me. "Now, get the coffee down, and let's head out. That truck's not going to drive itself out of the impound lot."

It was a horrible thought—my poor food truck with its colorful stripes sitting in a lot, surrounded by heaven alone knew which types of vehicles.

Bee and I finished our coffees, then headed out of the room and into the guesthouse proper, smiling at the host, Samantha, where she sat behind the reception desk with Trouble on her lap, purring. It was a scenic walk from there down to the wharf.

The entrance was gated, but those gates were open, and most of the jetties and docking spots were empty. Crates were stacked neatly to one side of a low-slung wooden building to the right, its door shut, and a fine layer of grime coating the windows on either side of it. Buoys hung off the walls, colorful or faded by the sun.

A few cars were parked outside the entrance, some of them shimmering in the sunlight. One in particular stood out. It was weather-beaten and old, rust pitting the hood near the windshield.

Owen's first words to me rang through my mind, as we stepped onto the wooden boards that led to multiple jetties, holding neatly stacked lobster traps or lengths of rope.

"Have you heard about the ghost on Springs Wharf?"

It was past time we got to the bottom of the confusing issue regarding Owen, the lobster boat, and the owner of the wharf. And the murder. Heavens, there was too much to investigate here.

We knocked on the office door before entering, me first, followed by Bee.

A man with graying hair and a vast belly sat behind a desk underneath the window, tapping his fingers on a laptop's keyboard. He looked up. "Sorry," he said. "We don't do private fishing tours."

"Oh. No, that's not what we came here for," I said, tucking my hands into the pockets of my woolen dress. "We wanted to speak to Mr. Dillington."

"What about?"

"Owen Pelletier."

The man narrowed his sea-green eyes at me. "Why?"

"We're interested," Bee said. "Apparently."

"Do you know where he is?" I asked. "It's pretty important."

The man sniffed. "You're looking at him."

"You're the owner of the wharf? Owen's boss?"

"Owner of the wharf, yeah. Boss, not really. Owen's boss was the owner of the boat he worked on. This wharf is privately owned, but we operate like a co-op. Folks come to fish here. I buy from 'em and sell to local restaurants or companies."

"Oh." I blinked. "Oh, so you didn't want to fire Owen?"

"No." Dillington ruffled his gray hair. "Where are you getting this from?"

I paused. I'd had a feeling that the chef at the restaurant had given me a garbled version of the truth. It seemed that gut instinct had been right. Dillington hadn't had it out for Owen, or, he didn't have the power to fire him. Short of kicking the company Owen had worked for out of the wharf entirely. Why had Miller lied?

Or did he just not know the truth himself?

"We were at the Lobster Shack last night," I said slowly. "And we overheard that you didn't want to supply lobster to the restaurant because of, well, of Owen."

"Firstly," Dillington said, raising a fat finger. "I don't see how that's any of your business nor why you think it's a good idea to question me about Owen and the Lobster Shack." He said the word 'idea' with a hard 'r'. "And secondly, the Lobster Shack is run by an idiot."

"Owen's uncle."

"Still an idiot. Always trying to make a deal, looking to buy lobster at reduced prices, sweeping in at the last moment to annoy us all with questions about why the lobsters seem smaller than usual this year." Dillington huffed out a breath. "Idiot. I'm not the only one who won't sell to 'im either. Most of every wharf don't want nothing do with the man."

So, Dillington hadn't hated Owen. Or he was pretending otherwise.

"You still haven't explained why you interrupted my working hours to talk to me about the Lobster Shack."

Bee and I looked at each other. "We're interested in Owen," I said, at last.

"You're interested in Owen." Dillington's eyes grew even narrower and then widened. "You! I know who you are. You're the woman he was meant to go on a date with. He bragged about it all morning before the boat went out. A beautiful brunette from out of town. That right?"

"Yes," I said. "I was the one who, uh, found him."

"Oh. Sorry about that. Can't have been a nice sight."

I shook my head. "We want to find out what happened to him, you know? It seems the right thing to do. Do you know anyone who might've..."

"What, wanted to kill the guy? Can't say that I do. Owen wasn't well-liked, but he wasn't a bad fisherman. He did right by his captain, and he worked hard." A frown wrinkled Dillington's brow. "Though, hmmm."

"'Though, hmmm?' Care to elaborate?" Bee asked.

"Well, see, Owen had been sick a lot, lately. Day before

he was murdered, he had to go home instead of going out on the boat, and that's a big deal in this business."

"What kind of sickness did he have?"

"No idea. Didn't ask. But my guess was it had something to do with his stomach."

Poisoning? Could it be that Owen had been poisoned before I even met him?

"Listen, ladies, my advice is you leave this to the cops. They'll figure out what really happened to Owen, and then we can put this behind us and get back to business. Murder's bad for tourism. And lobster fishing."

And that was it. We wouldn't get much more out of Dillington. But we had certainly gotten enough. As we walked back out of the wharf, I turned it over in my mind. The chef had lied. Dillington didn't seem to care much about the murder other than how it would affect business in town.

"Look at this," Bee said.

She stood next to the beat-up car in the street in front of the wharf, pointing to a slip of paper tucked beneath the windshield wiper.

I extracted it, carefully, and turned it over, flattening it out.

You'll regret this, Owen. I'll make it so you never forget me.

"It must be his car," Bee said, reading over my shoulder.

"Do you think...?"

"The note is from the murderer? It could be. It might be. Put it away, quick, before anyone sees. You give that to the walking walnut cop, and he'll only use it against you. Or he won't believe you."

I folded the note and tucked it into my pocket. It might've been the wrong thing to do, but it was our first real clue.

We hurried back down the road toward the guesthouse before anyone could stop us.

Nine

THE GUESTHOUSE WAS USUALLY FULL FOR dinner, but the murder had put a dampener on spirits. The lovely couple I had met in the hallway this morning had been rushing to pack their bags and leave the town, though they still had the time to smile and share a few kind words with me.

I sat at a table in the guesthouse's open-plan living room and dining area, a fire crackling merrily in the grate nearby. Bee had ordered a burger, and I'd gone for a lobster roll—thankfully, Dillington down at the wharf had no qualms about selling to the Oceanside Guesthouse, and Samantha was an absolute whiz in the kitchen.

The food hadn't arrived yet, and we had a chance to scan the relatively empty room and gossip, of course.

"It's interesting that the chef lied to you," Bee said,

drawing her coffee cup from the table and taking a sip. She had the odd habit of drinking coffee before bed and claimed it relaxed her.

"Interesting is one way of phrasing it." I kept my voice low.

A lone man sat in the corner next to the window, peering out at the ocean as the sun set, his chin balanced on his palm. We hadn't been introduced, and he likely didn't know anything about what had happened to Owen, but it was best to be cautious.

Particularly since the folks in Carmel Springs hadn't been friendly since the confiscation of the truck.

"Here we go!" Samantha swept out of the wooden swinging doors that led to the kitchen carrying two plates. "One chicken burger and one lobster roll." She set them down in front of us.

My mouth immediately started watering. The food smelled amazing, and Bee tucked in right away.

"Thank you so much," I said. "We're starving."

"You're very welcome." Samantha lingered, her gaze sweeping to Bee and then back to my face. "I heard about what happened to your food truck."

"Oh." *Oh no. Does she think I poisoned Owen too?* "Right."

"I just wanted to say I'm real sorry about that. There have been a lot of rumors flying around in town, and I don't want you to think that everyone has the same idea about you. That Detective Jones thinks he owns Carmel Springs. He's always been a wretched man."

"Thank you," I said. "I'm hoping we'll get the truck back soon."

"Me too. It's nice seeing it parked out at the beach. I heard you were serving hot cocoa."

"We were," Bee said, dabbing at the corners of her lips. "You know, before we were accused of being murderers."

The man at the window jerked and looked over at us.

"She's kidding," I said, waving at him. "We haven't done anything wrong."

Bee giggled.

"Enjoy your meal. You let me know if you need anything else. I've got a cheesecake in the fridge. I know it's probably nothing compared to the stuff you serve on your truck, but it's sweet and will fill the belly."

"I've always got a second stomach for dessert." Bee smiled at her.

And then we were left to eat our meal with the crackle of the fire for company—along with the occasional odd glance from the man at the window.

"I bet he thinks we did it now," I whispered.

Bee dragged a French fry through ketchup and grinned at me. "I'm struggling to care. Like I said, innocent until proven guilty. Opinions don't matter, darling."

"They do when you're in the food business."

"True. That's why I stick mostly to baking."

I finished off my lobster roll and struggled not to lick my fingers afterward.

We skipped out on the dessert and opted to head back to Bee's room instead, Trouble darting between my legs and purring on the way. The day had been full of excitement and questions, and I was tired after all of it.

I lowered myself into one of the armchairs, kicked up my feet on the coffee table, and let out a weighty sigh. "That's better. At least we can relax and talk about everything, now."

"Minus the prying ears and eyes." Bee nodded, sitting down as well.

"Can ears pry?"

"Small town ears should be able to." Bee tapped her manicured nails on the arms of her chair. "Speaking of ears, what *do* you think about the chef and the lies he dribbled into yours?"

"Dribbled?"

"Like sweet honey off the comb."

"I'm not sure," I said. "I don't know what to think. He might have been lying outright. Grace hinted that he'd gotten into a fight with Owen. Maybe he wanted to throw me off his scent."

"In which case, that's exactly the scent we should follow."

"I'll do whatever it takes to get the truck back. This has been my dream for the longest time, and if upsetting a few people will mean that I can—"

The floor in my bedroom creaked.

The door that led into the adjoining bathroom was open.

I paused, frowning. It couldn't be Trouble because the calico was already curled up on the end of the bed. Perhaps it was the guesthouse settling after a long day under the sun. Or the wind outside?

"What was that?" I whispered.

Bee shook her head.

Together, we got up. I took the lead, tiptoeing toward the bathroom door. *This is fine. It's probably nothing. Just a noise in an old house. But it's better to check to be sure.*

I opened the bathroom door, and Bee and I piled into the small tiled space. It was quiet as the grave—terrible turn of phrase to use in the situation, but there it was.

Another creak sounded in my room, and I stiffened.

There was definitely someone moving around in there.

I heated from head-to-toe, and my pulse raced. I crept forward, Bee right at my back, and pushed open the other bathroom door. The hinges creaked.

A figure stood framed in the moonlight next to my

bed. They were dressed in black and holding something that glinted in the darkness.

I gasped, shocks dancing over my skin.

"Hey!" Bee yelled. "What are you doing in—?"

The person took off running for the other side of the room, footsteps thumping on the floor.

"Stop right there!" Bee shot after the intruder, but I stayed put, bracing myself against the bathroom door.

It was a knife! They were holding a knife!

"Bee, wait!"

But it was already too late. My friend rushed from the room.

Ten

IT TOOK ME TWO GREAT GASPS OF BREATH BEFORE I could summon up the courage to rush out after Bee. I couldn't let her go out there on her own. What if the stranger turned on her? What if it was the murderer?

I hurried into the hallway. The lights were off, and my footsteps creaked. "Hello? Bee?" Something brushed against my leg, and I let out a squeal. A meow answered me. It was Trouble, his glowing yellow eyes peering up at me in the dark.

A door opened, and a light clicked on in the hallway.

"Ruby?" Samantha stood in her fluffy pink robe at the end of the hallway. "Is everything okay?"

"There was someone in my room. A stranger. With a knife, I think. And Bee went after him."

Samantha's jaw dropped.

"I have to find Bee. She might be in trouble."

The words had barely left my mouth when footsteps sounded on the stairs. I tensed up, waiting for the intruder to reappear, knife in hand.

Bee materialized on the landing, shaking her silver-haired head. "He's gone. Or she. Whoever it was, they got out before I could stop them."

"Well, thank heavens for that," I said. "What were you thinking, running after an intruder? What if they had turned on you? They had a knife."

"I'm not sure it was a knife, actually. It was silvery and metal, yes, but a knife?"

How could she possibly be so calm? I was still shaken from the interlude. "We have to call the police," I said. "They need to know what just happened." How could they possibly believe I was the murderer, or even Bee, when we'd almost been attacked?

"I'll make some tea," Samantha said. "To calm us down."

Another door opened in the hallway, and the male guest from downstairs stepped out, rubbing his eyes and wearing striped PJs. "What's going on?"

"It's Christmas morning," Bee said. "Santa Claus paid us a visit."

"There was a break-in," I said quickly since the guest

only blinked at the joke. "We're calling the police, and Samantha's going to make us some tea."

"And cookies." Samantha raised a finger. "I'll get right on it."

"And I'll call the police," Bee said with a glint in her eye.

I would've bet all the tea and cookies in the world that Bee would be speaking directly to Detective Jones and having a few harsh words with him.

Five minutes later, we were downstairs and seated in the living room, waiting for the police to arrive. The front door hadn't been left unlocked, but the intruder had jimmied it open to get inside. They had to have been desperate.

But who was it? And why had they been in my room? It was enough to make my skin crawl.

I hadn't seen much—but the intruder had been tall. Or maybe that had been my impression because of the fear. Their face had been hidden beneath a hood, and they'd been all in black. There was no way to tell whether they'd been male or female.

"Who do you think it was?" I whispered to Bee.

She sat next to me on the sofa, her brow furrowed. "I don't know, but I'd bet anything it was someone who didn't want us investigating what happened to Owen. Why else would they have broken into your room?"

I shuddered to think.

Another ten minutes passed before the police finally arrived. Detective Jones swaggered into the room, scowling when he spotted us.

"Hello, Detective Jones," Samantha said, rising from her seat next to the fire. "Can I get you anything? Some tea or a cookie or—"

"No." He put out a chubby-fingered hand.

Sam lowered herself back into the chair, and anger crawled up my throat. Good heavens, she'd only offered to be polite. Why was Jones so rude all the time?

"You," he said, pointing at me. "And you." His finger shifted to Bee. "Tell me what happened."

Bee opened her mouth, and I could almost see the acid gathered on her tongue.

I spoke before she could and broke down exactly what had happened. Meanwhile, two police officers examined the doors and then traipsed upstairs to my room. Detective Jones didn't even take notes, and he didn't seem concerned that we'd nearly been attacked.

"There's nothing we can do here," the detective said after my story had finished. "I can take your statement, but there's no evidence that will lead us to—"

"The latch on the door is broken," Bee said stiffly. "Samantha's going to have to fix that. There's definitive evidence that someone broke in."

"But none as to who it was." Jones shrugged. "We'll do what we can, but it's not much." And with that, he was done and gone.

"Well," Samantha said. "I'll have to call the locksmith tomorrow to get the door fixed." But the disappointment was thick in her tone. She had to be worried too. This was her business, and it was being messed around.

Because we were there.

If anything, this made me more determined to get to the bottom of what had happened to Owen. There was only one mystery I'd never solved. I wasn't about to add another one to that list.

Eleven

THE FOLLOWING MORNING WAS BRIGHT WITH watery sunshine. I'd gone for an early morning walk on the beach, feeling slightly lost now that I didn't have a truck to wake up to. As I made my way back to the guesthouse, my cheeks cold from the wind and my hair stiff from the salty air, I yawned.

Shoot, I'd hardly gotten any sleep last night. How was I supposed to when my room had been broken into? When the lead detective investigating a murder case happened to hate my guts? Or he believed that I'd poisoned the victim.

I came up the front steps of the guesthouse and sat on the porch swing outside, watching the street and the empty space where I'd parked my truck.

This was ridiculous.

I had to get it back. I had done nothing wrong.

"Why hasn't he taken me in for questioning yet?" I muttered.

The screen door creaked, and Bee emerged, pretty in a pink knit sweater and a pair of jeans and sneakers. "Who hasn't?"

"Oh, good morning." I shook my head. "I was just thinking about that detective."

Bee let out a low growl.

"If he really thinks I had anything to do with the murder, why hasn't he brought me in for questioning yet? It's strange."

"There are a lot of things he does that are strange," Bee said, leaning against the wooden balustrade. "Let's just say, I've had my fair share of experience with law enforcement, and the way he's been behaving has been unorthodox."

"Were you a police officer?" I asked.

"Not quite," Bee replied. "But I can see your investigative journalistic habits are operating at peak capacity."

"I can't help myself. I was up half the night trying to figure out who killed Owen and the next steps we should take."

I'd thought I'd put mysteries behind me when I'd bought the food truck—it had always been my dream to travel, to go on adventures and to avoid settling in one place for long, all while baking to my heart's content.

Bee looked out at the ocean, wriggling her lips from one side to the other. "We need another lead," she said. "My best guess is the truth lies in the details. Someone was clearly threatening Owen, and the only person we know who's had an actual fight with him is Miller, the chef from the Lobster Shack. Perhaps we'd better pay him another visit."

"Or the uncle."

"Owen's uncle?" Bee asked.

"Yes. I bet he'll know who would have wanted Owen dead."

"You mean apart from everyone in town who hated him?"

I laughed. "Apart from them, yes."

We went back into the guesthouse and grabbed two cups of coffee to go, right from Sam's machine with her handy Styrofoam cups and lids next to it, then headed out the door. The long walk down the street toward the pier refreshed me.

I loved walking, and even though this wasn't exactly how I'd planned to spend my time in Carmel Springs, it was nice to get some exercise. Working on the food truck definitely limited my time to walk or do anything else besides serving food. Or occasionally burning a cake, receiving a glare from Bee, and eating the leftovers at the end of a long day. Now, there was a recipe for weight gain if ever there'd been one.

We reached the pier and were greeted by narrow-eyed stares from a few of the locals in their stalls or shops. I took Bee's advice and ignored it, though it planted doubt in my belly. What if, when I got the food truck back, nobody came to buy any of our cakes, pies, or donuts? What if they avoided us because they believed I'd done it, no matter what the cops said?

It was a question I didn't want an answer to right now.

We strode up to the Lobster Shack. The glass front doors were slightly ajar, but there was no one inside.

Talk about a flashback.

I paused, a chill traveling down my spine.

"What is it?" Bee asked.

"Nothing. It's just too quiet."

"Well, it is the morning. Maybe the Lobster Shack doesn't open until later in the afternoon." Bee raised an eyebrow. "Looks like they're open."

"I don't know about that."

"There's only one way to find out."

Bee linked her arm through mine and guided me into the restaurant's interior.

It was quiet. The doors to the kitchen were shut, though the porthole windows let out the light from within. Had the chef come to set up early? That was what we did on the truck, and it made sense that a popular tourist att—

The low rumble of chatter cut across my thought.

Bee and I froze, her arm still linked with mine.

She nodded toward the door at the far end of the restaurant, next to a set of stairs that led to a second floor with a balcony.

"... think that's a wise idea." The words were low but audible.

I led the way forward this time. Who was it? Benjamin? The owner would come in early, of course, especially if he'd had troubles with the restaurant. The whole "no lobster" issue had to have hit hard.

"It doesn't matter what you think, Miller." The voice was rough as sandpaper.

Miller? The chef's in there with him.

"Listen, Ben, you don't have to believe me, but it's the best we can do at the moment. I ain't serving fake lobster to these folks. Most of the diners who come in here are locals. One bite, and they'll know it's not lobster."

"I think you're overestimating the local palate."

Miller fell silent, and Bee and I tensed. She tugged on my arm. Time to go. Or was it? We'd hardly heard anything other than Benjamin's willingness to cut corners to get what he wanted.

"Ben, I want the restaurant to do well too, but—"

Benjamin snorted inside the room. "If you'd wanted what was best for this restaurant, you would never have gotten into an argument with Owen in the first place."

A beat passed.

"He started it."

"And you finished it," Ben said.

My eyes widened. Was that an accusation?

"I did what I had to do. He wouldn't leave Hannah alone, boss. I wasn't about to take that lying down."

"And it didn't matter to you that your behavior would affect the restaurant. You knew that Owen would get you back for what happened, and that's why you—"

"Someone's coming," Bee whispered, squeezing her fingers into my forearm.

I'd been so drawn in by the conversation I hadn't heard the footsteps on the boardwalk outside. Quick as Trouble the cat, Bee and I made for one of the tables near the front and sat down.

Grace, the waitress, entered the restaurant and stopped just inside the doors. "What are you doing here?" she asked.

"We were hoping to have some breakfast," Bee said, her cheeks flush.

The server tucked her curly blonde hair behind her ears and released a long, low breath. "Oh," she said.

"Right. Sorry, we don't open until eleven today. You'll have to come back later."

We apologized our way out of the restaurant, smiling and laughing at our mistake. The restaurant's door shut behind us, and I took a breath.

"That was interesting," I whispered.

"More than interesting. Downright intriguing. It seems the chef was lying to you on purpose the other day."

And that made him even more suspicious.

"Come on, Ruby," Bee said. "Let's get back to the guesthouse and have some breakfast. We've got a long day of puzzling and clue-seeking ahead of us."

Twelve

I SAT ON THE PORCH SEAT, ADMIRING THE OCEAN view and occasionally scribbling a note on my pad. Bee had gone upstairs for an afternoon nap, but I couldn't shut my eyes for a second without seeing the lobster mallet.

It was a horrible vision to be taunted by, especially since it was supposed to be used on something delicious like a lobster in the shell. And it confused me too. Lobster made my mouth water. Murder did not.

I sighed and scanned my page again. I'd written all the names down and placed my clues next to them.

Owen Pelletier—Victim. Not exactly the most popular guy around. Murder by lobster mallet and poisoning? Sick in the days before his death. Why did the killer attack him and poison him as well?

"Odd," I muttered, turning the ideas over in my mind. Underneath Owen were the rest. The suspects.

Benjamin Pelletier—Owen's uncle. Owns the Lobster Shack. Blames Miller for the fact that there's no lobster and can't get it from any of the other suppliers. But does he hate Owen? Motive?

Chef Miller—Argued with Owen before his death. Definitely lied to me about Owen's relationship/connection to the Lobster Shack. Suspicious. Mentioned someone named Hannah? Owen won't stay away from Hannah?

Mr. Dillington—Owner of the wharf where Owen worked. Businesslike. Fairly nice guy and doesn't seem to care much about Owen's death. But... motive? None so far.

Relatives—Need to figure this out. Speak to the family?

So far, the most obvious player had to be Miller. He'd lied to me and clearly had a problem with Owen. But why? If only I could figure that part out.

I put my notepad and pen to one side. I needed a walk, some time to clear my mind and enjoy the view of the ocean. That would help me mull this over.

It had been a long time since I'd been faced with a set of clues I couldn't solve. Maybe the past few weeks on the food truck had blunted my investigative skills.

I got up and meandered down the porch steps to the side path that led toward the beach, between rough foliage and sand. It was quiet, apart from the odd car passing by once in a while and the natural sounds of the ocean. It would be so easy to forget, in this sweet small town, that there had been a murder.

"Don't be silly. No one's going to jump out at you," I whispered.

Apparently, I'd fully embraced my new habit of talking to myself. Perhaps it was due to the stress? Whatever the reason, I—

The crunching of footsteps on the path behind me sent a thrill through my center.

I paused.

The footsteps did too.

I glanced back, but there was no one there. There were plenty of places for someone to hide. The bushes on either side of the path, for instance.

Goosebumps lifted on my arms, and I shook my head.

"Don't be silly. You're just hearing things."

I set off again, and immediately, the footsteps crunched along behind me. They were offset with mine, too, so it was clear there was someone there.

Breathe, Ruby. You're going to be fine.

I'd done articles on big businessmen and oil magnates, criminals in prison and mob bosses who didn't want to be discovered. I'd seen my fair share of danger. I could handle this.

I can. Totally. I'm fine.

But panic sat in my throat.

What if it's the murderer?

I kept walking, listening hard. I quickened my pace, and the pursuer did too.

Instead of stopping, this time, I spun around to confront them.

My eyes widened.

The chef, Miller, stood there in his white uniform. He jerked on the spot and stopped walking.

"Why are you following me?" I asked.

He blinked. "I—uh, I wasn't. I'm just going for a walk on the beach."

I scoffed. "Please. I wasn't born yesterday. You're following me, and I want to know why."

Miller tucked his hands into his pockets and licked his thin lips. He shuffled on the spot. "Look, I—it wasn't anything bad. I just—" He huffed out a breath and removed his hands from his pockets again, thankfully without a lobster mallet in his grasp. "I heard around town that you were snooping and asking questions, talking about me, especially, and I wanted to know why."

That was it? Or was this yet more evidence that Miller had been involved in the murder? Why would he care that I'd asked questions if he was innocent?

"What did you fight with Owen about?" I asked.

The chef folded his arms. "Don't see how that's any of your business."

"I don't see how it's your business to be following me around. I'll happily report that to Detective Jones. It's suspicious behavior."

"No, no, you don't have to do that. See, now, I didn't mean any harm or nothing. I just wanted to—look, just stop asking questions about me, all right? It's starting to freak out Hannah, and I can't lose her. That would... well, it would be bad. Real bad."

"Who's Hannah?" I asked.

"My girl. She's, uh, well, she is Owen's sister. Owen was her brother. Shoot, I don't know how to put it."

Now, that was a lead. Owen's sister, Hannah. The same Hannah I'd overheard Miller talking about back at the Lobster Shack with his boss. "Why would you lose her?"

Miller hesitated. He scuffed his shoes on the gravel, looking down yet again. "Hannah, she's special to me. She don't like all the craziness that's been going on around here lately. And she don't like other women asking questions about me either."

I paused. Of course.

Miller had asked me on a date the other day at the restaurant. Meanwhile, he had Hannah, who was his girl-friend, waiting for him at home. Irritation gathered in my gut—there was nothing I despised more than a person who betrayed their significant other. But that wasn't my problem now.

"So look, just stop asking questions because she's starting to think you might like me. People like to spread rumors, y'know?"

Rumors or truths? I didn't doubt that Miller had enjoyed a few affairs in the past. Poor Hannah.

I have to talk to her. About her brother.

"I'll stop asking questions if you tell me the truth," I said. "Did you or did you not murder Owen Pelletier?"

Miller's bright eyes went round as donuts. "Of course, I didn't!" he snapped. "And how dare you say that to me? I wouldn't have... I didn't never... I—"

"Then why did you fight with him?" I asked, taking a single step toward the man.

Strangely, Miller stumbled back. As if I was the one who was truly intimidating in this situation. I sized him up.

"Look, I just. Fine! You want to know why? Fine. I'll tell ya. Owen was a piece of work. He flirted with all the women in the restaurant. He caused trouble with his uncle. And he was using his sister. Hannah's an angel, man, a real angel, and she deserved better than to have a lowlife brother hanging off her apron strings like she was his mom."

"So you took matters into your own hands."

"No," Miller said firmly. "I was over at Hannah's place, having a date and all, when Owen came home and started causing trouble. He'd brought lobsters with him, some he bought from work, and he wanted Hannah to stop our date and cook them for him. She said no. He flipped out." Miller took a breath, shaking his head at the memory. "He threw a lobster at her."

"He what?"

"He threw a lobster at Hannah."

"Good heavens."

"And that's when I lost my cool. I punched him right on the nose. Police were called out because it was a domestic disturbance. After that, well, all of a sudden the Lobster Shack couldn't get lobster anymore. Ben, the owner? He blames me for that."

So, either Dillington lied to me about why he wouldn't sell lobster to the Shack or Miller was lying, again.

"That's it, all right?" Miller took one step back, then another, raising his palms. "I did what I came to do. All I wanted was to ask you to stop with the—"

"Ruby!" The yell came from down the path, nearer to the guesthouse. "Ruby! Where are you?"

"I'm here," I called.

Bee appeared, jogging across the gravel toward me, her hair sticking up on one side and pillow creases imprinted into her cheek. She passed by the chef without taking any notice of him. Bee grabbed me by the arms, gasping for breath.

"Bee, what is it? What's wrong?"

"Don't. Ever. Make. Me. Run. Again."

She bent over, swiping at her forehead.

"What's going—?"

"It's the food truck," she said, a smile parting her lips, showing off the gap between her two front teeth. "It's back!"

Thirteen

AND THERE SHE WAS.

The apple of my eye. The cream on top of the cherry pie. Man, I'd gotten good at the whole rhyming thing in the last little while. It happened naturally whenever I was at my happiest. And right now, I was truly joyous.

The Bite-sized Bakery food truck was parked in front of the Oceanside Guesthouse again, sparkling beneath the afternoon sun, its pastel pink-and-green stripes merrier than I'd felt the past few days without it.

Detective Jones stood in front of it, his arms folded and one eye narrowed at us.

"It's back," I said.

"Told you so."

Bee wore a Cheshire Cat grin. Not even the detective's presence could put a damper on her good humor.

"Miss Holmes," the detective said, stomping forward and rolling his lips this way and that, as if he'd tasted something terrible and couldn't decide on where to spit it out. "I'm here to give back your vehicle. Here are the keys."

"About time," Bee growled. "Did you really think you'd find poison on that truck? If you did, you're meaner and dumber than a—"

"Bee." I placed a hand on her arm to stop the words. Just because Jones was annoying and definitely not our biggest fan, didn't mean we should provoke him. He was still a police officer and one who could put us away for antagonizing him. At least for the night.

"That's a wise decision," Jones said.

"Don't you worry about what's a wise decision or not."

"Bee," I repeated, then put out my hand to accept the keys to my truck.

Jones hesitated. He sniffed and then placed them in my palm. "This doesn't change anything," he said. "You'll stay out of the way, out of trouble, or I'll put you away for interfering in an ongoing investigation. Understand me? We don't like nosy out-of-towners in our Carmel Springs."

"Does that mean I'm no longer a person of interest in the case?" I asked.

Jones did the strange lip-rolling again, back and forth, back and forth. "Everyone's a person of interest until they're not." And then he clomped off down the road to a waiting cruiser, his partner or just another officer, seated behind the wheel. The car sped off the minute he was inside.

"A bit of a cowboy, isn't he?" I asked.

"Not the word I would have used."

"I get the feeling the word you would have used is one that shouldn't be spoken out loud."

"You always were intuitive."

I laughed and slung my arm through Bee's, squeezing it in my excitement. "We've got the truck back! I don't believe it."

"I do," Bee said. "Though, I'm sure Jones held it as long as possible just to inconvenience us. Hobbit of a man."

"That's an insult to hobbits."

"True. Hobbits are industrious, at least. And Jones is..."

"Wait, wait, wait," I said. "If we start this, I know I'll be stuck with you mocking him all day long."

"I don't see anything wrong with that."

I swung the keys in my hand and caught them against my palm, the jangle pleasant in my ears. "May I point out that it's probably not a good idea to upset the police in town? We do want to serve our customers, after all."

"Serve them?" Bee asked. "I don't see why. This town

has been nothing but terrible since we arrived, apart from Samantha. And the kitty, Trouble. And maybe that waitress at the Lobster Shack. We should leave."

"Leave?" I frowned.

It didn't feel right to just run off. Particularly not in the middle of a murder investigation. Though, to be fair, it wasn't my murder to investigate.

"Yes, we should leave. If Jones doesn't care whether we leave or not..."

"He didn't say that. He didn't confirm it."

Why was I so hesitant? It felt like unfinished business to run off without having solved the case. A part of me was desperate for the truth. After all, the last mystery I'd encountered had gone unsolved, and that had been personal. It had hurt me. Deeply.

I paused, stroking my thumb over my bottom lip. "Well, whatever happens, we need to clean this truck before we go anywhere. I'm not going to serve our treats out of it without giving it a proper wipe-down."

"Good point. Who knows where Bilbo poked and prodded while we were gone," Bee said.

THE EARLY AFTERNOON SOON TURNED TO LATE, as Bee and I cleaned the truck inside and out. Bee opted to take care of the interior, determined to scour all evidence of the rude "Tweedledum" before night fell. Every now and again, she'd let out a grunt at something or the other. A few times, she had popped her head out the truck's window to complain about a pot that wasn't stacked correctly or a surface that had clear smudges on it.

"I'll be right back," I said.

I collected my bucket and walked around the side of the guesthouse to fill it with water from the outside faucet. Samantha had been kind enough to lend me all the things I'd need to spruce up the truck.

And then tomorrow?

I wasn't sure what we'd do yet. My stomach clenched at the thought of leaving Carmel Springs. I liked the town, but that wasn't it. I wanted to understand why Owen had been murdered. It was about more than just the truck now.

There was a mystery to be uncovered. A murderer to be brought to justice.

I finished filling up my bucket, heaved it up with both hands then made my way back to the truck. There was something cathartic about cleaning. Scrubbing away layers of dirt to reveal the fresh colors beneath made me happy, in a way.

I set my bucket down, placed my fists on my hips, and studied the truck.

"Hey!" The shout had come from the street. "Hey, you!"

I backed up and scanned the street.

A fiery redheaded woman strode across the street, her hair flying out behind her. She was taller than me and, judging from the size of her arms, a great deal stronger. She wore a tank top and a scowl. Both scared me.

"Hello," I said, trying for friendly but falling short at anxious. "I'm sorry, but we're not open at the moment. If you come back tomorrow—"

"I'm not here for the cakes," the woman snapped, coming to a stop in front of me.

Bee popped her head out of the window at the noise. "Good heavens, it's the Green Giant. Except red."

"I don't think this is the time, Bee," I said, trying to keep my voice low.

Clearly, this lady wasn't in the best of moods.

"You're right. I'm not in the mood," the woman snapped. "I came here to warn you to stay away from my man." She jabbed a finger in my direction. "I've had enough of people like you. Women who can't keep their hands to themselves."

"Pardon me?" I asked.

"How rude," Bee said, shaking her head. "Now, I don't take back my Green Giant comment."

"You know what I'm talking about."

"I really don't. Look, who are you?" I asked.

The woman huffed a breath. "Hannah," she said. "My name is Hannah, and don't lie to me. I heard all about you flirting with Miller at the Lobster Shack."

My eyebrows rose. This was Owen's sister? It would pay for me to get on her good side, but it looked as if that ship had already sailed. "I'm not interested in Miller, I assure you. All I want to do is serve my cakes and—"

"Whatever," Hannah hissed. "You stay away from him, do you hear me? You've been warned."

She spun on her heel and stormed back down the street.

"Well," I said, blinking. "That went well."

"About as well as anything else has gone this week," Bee replied. "Interesting, though. It seems Miller's a flirt."

I frowned. Something about this seemed important, but I couldn't put my finger on what it was. It had to do with the case, with Owen, with the fights between Miller and Owen. Of course, Hannah wouldn't have been involved in those unless I counted the lobster-tossing incident.

But no, it was something else. If only I could figure out what it was...

"Don't let her bother you. Tomorrow, Carmel Springs will be in our rearview mirror. We'll find another town in Maine with lobster rolls and friendly folks," Bee said and wagged her rag at me. "Come on. Let's finish up. Samantha said she was making steak tonight! And roast potatoes."

"You had me at steak."

I set to work, but my thoughts stayed on Owen and the murder.

Had Hannah been involved?

Fourteen

I SIGHED AND PLACED MY FISTS ON MY HIPS, examining my bag and the neatly folded shirts and pants I'd tucked inside it. Trouble wound between my ankles, purring and occasionally batting them as if he could persuade me to change my mind.

Then again, I hadn't exactly made it by myself.

"You know," Bee said, lugging her bag behind her. "I think that's the fiftieth time you've sighed this morning, and it's only eight a.m."

"Breakfast in an hour. We could stay and have some waffles. Sam said she was more than happy to—"

"Hmmm."

"What?"

"Now, granted, I don't know you very well yet, Ruby, but from what I've seen so far, you don't strike me as the person who settles down," Bee said. "You seem like the type who wants to keep moving, you know, given that you own a food truck and you wanted a baker who was happy to traverse the country indefinitely."

"What's your point?" I asked, holding back another sigh.

"That you don't want to leave. And that's odd."

I sat down next to my suitcase. "It's the murder," I said. "I can't stop thinking about it and wondering who did it. And why? All the clues are caught up in my head, swirling around and around and—"

Bee came forward and placed a hand on my shoulder. "Ruby, dear, it's not your place to investigate it or solve it. I understand that you were a journalist before this, but you've moved on from that. And we should move on from this town and go to the next one. After all, there are plenty of quaint coastal towns to visit around these parts."

"I like Carmel Springs," I said. "Most of the people are lovely, and the restaurants and food are great. And the view..."

"I like it too. But this is for the best."

Bee was right, of course. The murder hadn't been solved yet, and the customers in Carmel Springs likely wouldn't flood to the food truck if we did open it again. Not after the whole "poisoned cake" rumor that had spread through the town.

"We're off on our next adventure now," Bee said.

And that brought me to my feet. I had left Daniel in the past, the mystery of where he had gone and why he had left me too, and I could do the same with this one. I zipped up my bag, lifted it off the bed, and then bent and scratched Trouble behind the ears.

"All right," I said. "I'm ready."

We headed downstairs and gave Samantha a hug good-bye. She asked us to sign the guest book and then presented us with a polished seashell as a souvenir from our time at the guesthouse.

"Drive safe," Samantha called as we exited the front door and thunked our bags down the steps toward the...

Bee stopped dead.

I gasped, my hands flying to my mouth.

The Bite-sized Bakery food truck had been trashed. The windows had been broken, the tires punctured so the rubber had puddled against the asphalt, and the pink-and-green stripes had been spray-painted with a threatening message.

Back off.

You're next.

I trembled on the spot, unable to think or even speak.

"No," Bee said next to me. "No, no, no."

"How? Why?" I whispered, shaking my head.

The front door of the guesthouse opened, and another gasp rang out, this one from Samantha. "Oh no."

Bee turned. "Dear, would you be so kind as to call the police?"

"Right away."

The door clicked shut again.

I stumbled back and sat down heavily on the bottom step, my eyes pooling with unshed tears. "Why? Who would do this?"

"I don't know," Bee said. "But it looks like we'll have the time to find out. We can't go anywhere like this."

Our time at Carmel Springs was far from over, it seemed. And I doubted Detective Jones would be overly enthused about helping us figure out who had done this.

You're next. It says that I'm next. Does that mean...? Could it have been the murderer? But no, why would they do that? It would only draw more attention to themselves and the case if that were true. So it had to have been the same person who'd broken into my room in the guesthouse.

Or... No, surely not.

Hannah.

She had warned me to stay away. Perhaps she'd decided to act on that warning after all.

Motion blurred around me as I sat staring at the truck —it was meant to be my freedom. My dream. And it had been reduced to nothing but a mess of threats and shattered glass.

Someone tapped me on the shoulder, and I looked up.

"Here," Samantha said. "Have some hot cocoa. You'll feel better soon. I'm so sorry this has happened, Ruby. I don't understand it. I didn't hear a thing last night."

"Thank you." I accepted the mug and took a sip of the bolstering sweetness.

It didn't matter *that* it had happened, but *why* it had happened.

The police arrived, but I barely paid them any mind, save to answer their questions and give my statement. My thoughts whirled around the possibilities, and eventually, a certainty settled in my gut.

If I was going to stay in Carmel Springs, by no choice of my own, I'd find the killer and the person who'd trashed my truck, whether they were one and the same or not.

Fifteen

Finding Hannah Pelletier's address had been as easy as a trip down to the Lobster Shack and a chat with our favorite server Grace. She'd been more than happy to dish the address and a little bit of dirt. Namely, Hannah was a total loon and had threatened countless women around Carmel Springs because she was as jealous as the day was long. And that Miller happened to be a serial cheater, which definitely didn't help the cause.

None of that mattered. I had my suspicions that Hannah was the one who had destroyed, or tried to destroy, my food truck. And that meant it was high time I paid her a visit. Even though she was huge and scared the dreams and hopes out of me.

I'd tucked the threatening note from Owen's car into my pocket, just in case I could somehow find something of

Hannah's to match it with. It was a long shot, of course. Perhaps Hannah would recognize the handwriting? Or know who had been threatening her brother? Or maybe, it was her. And she had trashed the truck and killed her brother.

Now, there was a horrifying thought or three.

"You know," Bee said as we strolled down the sidewalk, past quaint stores on Main Street, nodding to the occasional passerby. "You could have just checked the phonebook."

"There are still phone books? I thought we'd transitioned to the digital age."

"The youth of today." Bee rolled her eyes. "Of course, there are phone books. I bet Samantha has one in the office at the guesthouse."

"Yes, but I highly doubt that the phonebook would have gossiped with me about Hannah and Miller."

"I didn't realize that gossip was high on your agenda of phonebook requirements," Bee said.

"It's not. But you know what I mean. I like things to be in person, you know? It's much easier to unravel the details of a person's character face-to-face."

"That's only slightly creepy."

I grinned. "Only slightly. It's a bad habit I picked up during the journalist years."

"You mean BFT?"

"BFT?"

"Before Food Truck. I figured we should create acronyms since we talk about it a lot. The past. The future. The mystery." Bee wiggled her fingers at me like she could cast a spell.

"All right then," I said. "BFT and AFT. That works."

"So BFT, you were used to talking to people face-to-face and squeezing them for information."

"True," I said. "And most of them were filled with it like a delicious jelly donut is filled with a raspberry jelly center."

"Hmm." Bee adjusted her handbag on her shoulder as we turned into a side street. "I'm not sure whether I'm hungry or disgusted."

I chuckled and shaded the screen of my phone, following the GPS directions toward Hannah's street. She lived at number 13—how ominous—on Sunset Road. The houses on either side were tucked back between trees or at the backs of long lawns with garden ornaments. The people there kept the esthetic quaint, in line with the rest of Carmel Springs.

Finally, we reached Hannah's house and proceeded up a stone path toward a gated front door flanked on either side by two potted plants.

"Seems like Hannah's doing well for herself," I said. "This is a nice house."

"I'm assuming she extorts people for a living, what with those massive arms and that thunderous voice."

"Be nice."

"A difficult request for me. When someone upsets my friend, I can't help being just as mean back. An eye for an eye."

"Whatever happened to turn the other cheek?" But I was touched that Bee considered me enough of a friend she felt it necessary to stick up for me. I hadn't had many friends like that, not at work, at least, and those friends I'd had before Daniel... well, they were all gone. Married or with kids. And I was the odd one out.

I pressed the buzzer next to the front door, and merry chimes sounded inside. We waited. Nothing happened.

"Maybe she's not home?"

"Maybe," I said and pressed the buzzer again. "I guess I should have asked Grace where she works instead of where she lives. That's an oversight on my part. Oh, shoot, now what?"

"Are you looking for that ginger tree?" A croaking voice traveled from the garden next door.

Bee and I spun toward it.

"Sorry?" I asked, shading my eyes from the sun.

The woman was old and bent double, grasping at the hedge that separated her yard from Hannah's. "You heard me right," she crowed. "The ginger tree. Hannah Pelletier.

Never liked the girl or her brother. Always fighting. Always making noise and disturbing the neighborhood. The bad type, those two. Glad at least one of them is gone now."

I was at a loss for words. Bee was too.

"She's not home, see? Hannah. She's at work."

"Oh," I said, my brain finally clicking on. "Where does she work?"

"At the community college. Teaches a baking class," the woman said. "Not that she knows all that much about baking. That brother of hers had a sweet tooth of note, and word on the street is he never wanted to eat what she baked. Thought it was disgusting. I overheard them fighting about it."

My heart skipped a beat.

Baking? Hannah was a baker?

And Owen was sick the day before he died. Poisoning? Could it be?

"You be careful of that Hannah, dears," the woman said with a cackle. "She seems nice, but she's evil-made flesh. I'd bet my last penny that she's the one who did it. Killed her brother. Flotsam and jetsam." She snorted and spat into Hannah's yard.

Bee and I recoiled as one.

"Um, well, thank you," I said. "For telling us all of that. We're going to go now."

I clasped Bee's arm, and we turned away from the crone and hurried back down the stepping stones.

"You be careful of her," the woman shouted after us. "You watch your backs. Hannah Pelletier is not a woman to be trifled with."

Sixteen

THE COMMUNITY COLLEGE WASN'T TOO FAR OFF Main Street. It was a series of flat brick buildings separated by concrete paths and grassy knolls. The walk over hadn't taken us too long, but both Bee and I were aching for a meal and a little something to drink.

We grabbed a bottle of water and a seriously underwhelming lobster meat sandwich from the cafeteria. Then, we sat on one of the wrought-iron benches to wait. The office receptionist had told us that the baking class in Hall 7B would let out in about ten minutes.

"This is nice," I said, tipping my head back to accept the sunlight on my face.

"I assume you're not talking about the sandwiches."

"No, just being here. Look at the trees." The leaves had turned to reds, yellows, and oranges, and each time the wind blew, a few trickled down to land on the grass. "It's fall. The wind is nippy, but the air seems full of…"

"Murder?"

"Promise," I corrected. "And spice. And pumpkin."

"And mediocre lobster sandwiches." Bee swiveled and peered back at the wooden doorways to the hall. "I wonder what they're baking in there. It can't be anything good."

"Why do you say that?"

"My mother was a baker too, you know, it's where I got the passion from, and she always said that when you're too sour or bitter, that comes out in the food," Bee replied. "Now, I know I have my moments, especially when it comes to meanies like Detective Jones and this Hannah woman, but it's people who are sour all the time that don't bake well. Things flop that shouldn't. Cakes taste strange. The frosting is never the right consistency."

"A baking conspiracy theory," I said. "I like it. Maybe we'll get to uncover the mystery behind that on our adventures."

Bee chuckled and finished off the last of her sandwich, her smile turned upside down as she chewed. "I mean, really. There's more to life and lobster than mayonnaise. The bread is soggy."

The hall's doors finally opened, and Bee and I rose, disposing of our trash in a can a few feet away.

Crowds of students came out, most of them wearing

aprons stained with chocolate or checking notes as they walked. It was a nice idea. I'd taken a very brief baking course before starting my business venture. However, I was still a novice in comparison to Bee.

Hannah appeared among the students, marching out with a scowl twisting her features and her red hair tied in a bun atop her head. She was seriously tall, but "ginger tree" wasn't a fair label for her. She was an attractive woman in her own way. Handsome.

Bee and I hurried across the lawn and met her a short way from the hall doors.

"Hello," I said and gave a wave. "How are you?"

"Are you crazy?" Hannah asked.

"Not since I last checked."

"You came here? To my place of work? I warned you to stay away from me."

Her fingers twitched at her sides.

"Actually, you warned me to stay away from Miller, who, by the way, is not my type." I cleared my throat delicately. "And I'm not here because of that. I'm here because of my truck."

"Huh?"

"My food truck," I said, my nerves building.

It was one thing to plan a confrontation, but to actually do it... well, my palms had grown sweaty.

"You know, the one you trashed?" Bee stood with her arms folded.

"I have no idea what you're talking about. But I do know that stalking is illegal. I'm going to report you for this."

"Look," I said, "I know we didn't get off to a great start, but I need to talk to you. Someone trashed my truck, and if it wasn't you, then it might be the person who murdered your brother."

Hannah paused. She fiddled with her apron, untying the strings, removing it, and then tucking it over one arm. Every motion was precise, and she didn't meet my eye. "My brother... I hate to say it, but he got what he asked for. He made an enemy of just about everyone in town, and though he was my blood, and the Lord knew I loved him, I have to be honest with myself about what happened. He brought it on himself."

That was a terrible sentiment. Blaming the victim. It got my back up, but I took a breath. "I just want to figure out who's been threatening me."

"Apart from you," Bee put in.

Hannah patted her apron repeatedly. "Owen was threatened, too," she said. "A lot. Someone slathered his whole windshield with fat the once."

"With fat?" Bee gaped.

"With fat. Pig fat. It was disgusting. He got notes, and our house was broken into, as well."

"He lived with you?" I asked.

"Before the incidents, yes. I couldn't handle living with him anymore. He really knew how to rub a person the wrong way, and it didn't matter to him that I was his sister. He would make me as unhappy as possible. He would complain about my cooking, even though he couldn't cook or bake himself, and he would leave the house a mess. He played loud music, and he would have woman after woman come over to the house on dates and make me cook the meals for them!"

I struggled not to blush. Owen had asked me out on a date. "So you kicked him out."

"Yes, I did. Two weeks ago. I think he was sleeping in his car, but he brought it upon himself." Hannah threw up her hands. "I'm not going to feel guilty about it. Owen was a meanie. Our own mother wasn't talking to him, for heaven's sake."

Another woman exited the doors behind Hannah, and I did a double-take. It was Grace, the waitress, walking across the lawn toward us.

"Sorry to interrupt," she said, tucking blonde hair behind her ears, which were big. "I forgot to hand in my assignment." She thrust a piece of paper with a recipe written on it toward Hannah. "Sorry, Ms. Pelletier."

"Fine." Hannah waited until Grace had walked off before turning back to us. She chewed on the corner of her lip. "We should talk. About Owen. You're welcome to come back to my house. I've got some cookies left over from my morning baking session."

"Are you sure?"

This was quite a change from threatening my life.

What if the cookies have been poisoned?

I didn't have to eat them.

"Yes." Hannah shifted her weight from one foot to the other. "Yes. I'm sure. Follow me."

Seventeen

THE MINUTE WE ENTERED THE WARM, SUN yellow kitchen in Hannah's house, my mind was set at ease. There was no way she was the murderer. A person who baked such delicious-smelling cookies couldn't possibly have an evil, murdering bone in their body.

Still, I seated myself at the square table and waited for Hannah to take a bite of a chocolate-chip cookie before I did.

Hannah crunched on it, a frown wrinkling her brow, and Bee and I helped ourselves to a cookie each.

They were delicious. None of the sour bitterness in Hannah's personality had dripped into the batter, despite Bee's fears. The cookies were moist and sugary, the chocolate chips melted and rich, and I gobbled up two before forcing myself to stop and focus on the task at hand.

Getting to the bottom of what had really happened to Owen. And my truck. My poor, poor truck.

"You wanted us to come back here with you?" I asked.

"Yes. I didn't want you to run off thinking that I was the one who hurt Owen," Hannah said.

"Why would we think that?"

"Oh, come on, you don't think I've heard the rumors? Everyone gossips in this town. It's a way of life, and the old hag, Mrs. Maggert, next door? She's no exception. She's been telling anyone who will listen that I'm the one who killed Owen. As if I would do something like that to my own brother. It's disgraceful."

"But you didn't get along," Bee said.

"Of course, we didn't. Like I said, Owen was a pain in the neck. He did what he wanted and didn't care who he hurt in the process."

"Do you know who might've wanted to hurt him back?"

It was the politest way I could put it.

"Plenty of people," she replied. "Nobody liked him. Nobody wanted him around. I think even the captain of his boat hated Owen, but Owen was good at what he did, so there was no point in firing him. Even my—"

The chimes from the doorbell tinkled, and Hannah excused herself from the table to check who it was.

"What do you think?" I asked Bee.

"I don't know. Her cookies taste good. She can't be as mean as I thought."

"No, I meant about the murder. About Owen and the threats and—"

Voices traveled down the hall, and I perked up, listening hard. A man spoke in the house, a rumbling that was familiar.

An elderly man, who looked a lot like Owen, entered the kitchen. He wore a plaid shirt and shrugged off his coat as he entered, his bright blue eyes sweeping over the kitchen. He spotted us and stopped. "I didn't realize you kept the company of murderers, Hannah."

"Don't be melodramatic, Uncle Ben," she replied easily and took her place at the table again. "I invited these women to join me for coffee and cookies. I didn't do the same for you."

"You kicking me out?" Benjamin asked.

"Keep causing trouble, and I will."

Benjamin grunted and headed to the fridge. He jerked open the door, brought out a carton of milk, and then drank directly from it.

Bee recoiled. I didn't blame her.

"Don't mind him," Hannah said. "He comes for dinner on Thursday nights. Gives him a break from his failing restaurant."

"Don't get me started, girl," Ben replied, wiping his mouth with the back of his hand.

Clearly, there was no love lost in this family. "We didn't mean to interrupt," I said.

"You're not. Now, where were we? Talking about who might have hated Owen enough to kill him."

Benjamin choked on milk, and a little sprayed out of his nostrils.

"For heaven's sake, Benjamin, contain yourself," Hannah snapped.

Benjamin cleaned himself up over the kitchen sink. "You're talking about Owen?"

"Who hated him," Hannah replied.

"Sheesh. I just talked to about fifty of 'em. Everyone hated the kid. Even I wasn't a fan. He caused trouble. Too much trouble."

Benjamin's eyes shifted toward Hannah, and his expression changed to one of concern. It was gone a second later, but I was sure I had seen it and that something was amiss. Something that involved Hannah.

"Did you ever see anyone threatening him?" I asked. "In person?"

"You mean apart from Miller?" Benjamin asked.

"That was different. Miller was protecting my honor."

"Oh, right," I said. "The lobster event."

The Pelletiers stared at me.

"What?" Hannah asked. "The what?"

"The lobster event. Miller told me he had to protect your honor when Owen threw a lobster at your face."

Hannah shook her head. "I have no idea what you're talking about."

"Are you sure?" I asked. "Miller told—"

"Miller likes to tell stories," Benjamin cut across my words. "It's part of who he is as a person. Listen, are you ladies going to finish those cookies anytime soon? I'm starving. I'd like to get my dinner done before five." He checked his watch.

I hesitated. "Just one last thing." I reached into my pocket and drew out the threatening note we'd found on Owen's car. "Do you know who might have written this?"

Hannah took it from me and scanned it. A frown wrinkled her brow.

"What?" Bee asked. "What is it?"

Hannah got up and walked to the kitchen counter where she'd dropped off the homework assignments she had to grade for the baking class. She brought them back, plopped them on the table, and began rifling through them.

Benjamin shrugged and rooted around in the fridge for something else to eat.

Bee and I shifted, sitting on the edges of our seats.

"I think..." Hannah removed one of the papers from the pile. "Yes. This is the same. I'd recognize it anywhere. I've been tutoring these students for over a year now." She placed the paper in front of us and then slid the threatening note into place on top of it. "See? The curl of the letters? It's the same, right?"

She was right. It didn't take a handwriting expert to recognize the similarities between what was on the page and the note. It was a recipe, scrawled out hastily, the edges of the page crumpled.

"Whose is it?" I asked.

Hannah shifted the note aside.

The student's name had been written across the top of the page.

Grace Allen.

"The waitress?" Bee asked. "But that doesn't..."

I didn't hear the rest of the sentence.

Grace.

The same Grace who had given us information on Miller. Who had served us food. Who took a baking class! Of course. Hadn't the lady next door said that Owen had a sweet tooth? After all, he'd come to my food truck before work in search of something sweet to eat.

And Owen had been sick for days before he'd died.

Grace had been feeding him baked goods. This had to be it.

I scraped my chair back, and the kitchen fell quiet.

"Ruby?" Bee asked. "Are you all right?"

"We have to go. Now."

"Where to?"

"The Lobster Shack."

Eighteen

"YOU'RE SURE YOU WANT TO DO THIS?" BEE asked as we charged onto the pier. "I've already called the police, you know. Detective Hobbit-face says he will find Grace and bring her in for questioning. From there, it's only a few short searches away from the truth." She paused, patting me on the forearm. "We don't have to go to the Lobster Shack. And Benjamin said she would be on her shift within the hour. Do we really want to run into the murderer?"

"We're not even sure she is the murderer," I said, but the words tasted of a lie.

Grace was definitely the one who'd killed Owen. She'd been a baker. She'd potentially poisoned him, but why? That was what got to me. Why had she done it? And why with the lobster mallet? Had the poison she'd used not been effective enough?

And why had Owen invited me to the restaurant when it had been closed?

Bee jogged along beside me, her sneakers squeaking on the pier's wooden boards. It was just past four, and from what Benjamin had said, the restaurant had been closed all day. He'd been avoiding serving people because he still didn't have a lobster supplier.

But the restaurant opened at five. This was the time to talk to her, figure out what had happened, and, if necessary, make a citizen's arrest.

My nerves bubbled and boiled.

"She might not be there yet," I said.

"Then why are we going?" Bee asked.

"I don't know. It just feels like the right thing to do."

We hurried past the late shoppers on the pier, drawing a few odd looks here or there because of how we rushed. Or maybe it was my pink cheeks and wild eyes. I felt a little crazed.

I had to know why. That was the point. I'd always wanted to understand why people did things, whether bad or good—it was part of the reason I'd become a journalist in the first place.

We finally reached the Lobster Shack and found the

front doors unlocked. We entered, and my heart got caught in my throat, pattering away frantically.

"Hello?" I called.

"We should leave this to the police, Ruby," Bee whispered. "It's only going to cause more trouble if we get involved. Trust me, I know how these types of things work."

How did she know? That was a question for another time.

"We'll be fine." It was my stubborn streak. I couldn't help myself. I had to know the truth! "Hello?" I called again.

But the interior of the restaurant was eerily silent. The lights were on overhead, the tables still with the chairs upturned atop them. The bar was empty, too, a few glasses stacked atop the polished wood surface, and the view out of the windows—the sun sinking toward the ocean—was idyllic.

"I mean, honestly. I haven't exactly been the most trusting of the detective," Bee continued, "but we have bigger cakes to bake. Quite literally. The truck isn't going to fix itself."

"We'll worry about the truck later. It's no use fixing it up if the murderer is just going to come back again to break into my room or—" I cut off, frowning.

Grace wasn't particularly tall. And the person who had broken into my room had definitely been tall.

I shook the thought out of my head. "Hello?"

The kitchen doors opened. Miller appeared, wearing his chef's whites and a hat. He took a step and then stopped at the sight of us.

"I'm not supposed to talk to you," he said, shying backward.

"I know, I know, but it's fine. We spoke to Hannah, and she's not worried anymore. Is Grace here?" I asked, looking around.

"No, the servers won't arrive for another half hour."

My shoulders sagged.

Miller took a step forward, dragging the chef's hat off his head and revealing his glistening golden locks beneath. It looked as if he'd had an accident with a bottle of hair gel. "Why do you want to see Grace?" he asked, his voice thin.

"Because she murdered Owen," I said without thinking.

"Ruby."

"Bee?"

"You probably shouldn't have said that."

Miller had gone pale as his uniform. "She-she what?"

"She murdered him." There was no use crying over spilled milk. Perhaps I'd bathe in it like Cleopatra instead. "We think."

"That's... that's impossible. Grace wouldn't do that."

"How can you be so sure?" I asked.

"Because she was—she just wouldn't do that. Grace is a good person. She's an amazing person. She—"

I gasped. "You're having an affair with her."

Miller bowed his head, looking off to one side. No wonder poor Hannah was so jumpy about other women near Miller. He was as flirty and duplicitous as the gossip in town said. "Ain't none of your business who I date."

"That's why you were fighting with Owen," I said, on a roll now. "Not because he threw a lobster at Hannah. That was a front. A fake story. Because you didn't want anyone to know the truth. You were having an affair, and Owen and Grace..." I got lost, blinking. "Owen flirted with Grace. He always did that with the servers, right?"

"Yeah." Miller barely spoke the word.

"And you two got into an argument."

"It ain't none of your business!"

"But it's true," I insisted, as Bee placed her hand on my arm and tried to tug me away. "So, let me piece this together. Okay? Owen had been flirting with Grace. You got angry and fought with him because of that. And you... you didn't like him either because..." But I couldn't quite piece it together.

If Owen had been flirting with Grace, why had Grace poisoned him? Was it out of sheer anger because he'd dared try to ask her out on a date? But that didn't make sense, either. And the lobster mallet? How did that factor into it all?

There was something missing.

The only thing I was sure about was that Miller definitely didn't want me to know the truth. And that he'd been lying.

I charged across the dining area toward him. Bee hurried along beside me.

"Ruby, you're as stubborn as a mule. Leave this to the police."

The mention of the cops drained even more blood from Owen's face. "You called the police?" he asked. "Why would you do that?"

"Because Grace deserves to be brought to justice," I said. "She was poisoning him. Did you know?"

"No, I swear, I didn't know it." Miller wet his lips.

But I didn't quite believe him. There was something in his eyes, a glint that was neither fearful nor ashamed. Had Miller been involved somehow? Had he...?

The door to the restaurant opened behind us, letting in a rush of cold air.

"Grace," Miller said quietly. "You're here."

"I couldn't let you deal with these two on your own, now, could I?"

Nineteen

ICE DROPPED INTO MY BELLY.

Grace was there. She entered the restaurant calmly and shut the door behind herself with an ominous click.

"I did mention that we should have left this to the police," Bee whispered.

"Thank you, that's a very helpful note. I'll bear it in mind."

Bee didn't smile, but she did slip her hand into mine and squeezed my fingers briefly. I took strength from the gesture and the fact that multiple windows looked out on the pier. I knew if we stalled Grace for long enough, Detective Jones would surely arrive and stop anything untoward from going down.

Assuming he did arrive.

What if he'd decided that Bee's call had been a hoax or that he didn't want to believe us? Or... any number of other horrible eventualities I didn't want to confront now.

I took a step back, and Bee did the same, her arms now at her sides.

If only we'd thought to bring my mace with us. But what would that help? Grace might have a weapon hidden on her person.

"You couldn't just butt out, could you?" Grace asked.

"I'd like to point out that represents a certain degree of irony coming from you," Bee replied. "You were the one feeding us information."

"Feeding them information? What's that about? Grace?" The chef rounded the bar, lifting a lobster mallet from behind it.

If I'd thought my stomach was icy before, it was nothing compared to the Antarctic situation going on in there now.

Of course. Why hadn't I considered it before?

They'd worked together.

"Why?" I asked. "Why did you team up to kill Owen?"

"We didn't," Grace replied. "I didn't really want to hurt Owen. I just wanted to make him a bit sick, you know? Because he'd cheated on me. Just a little bit of revenge. I didn't mean for it to go as far as it did or... I don't even know how it happened. I hadn't given him any baked goods for a day before he died." Her gaze switched to Miller and then back to me. "Owen was..."

"Just say it," Miller snapped. "It's too late. They already know too much. This is your fault, Grace. You're just as culpable as I am now. The deaths of these two women will be on your hands now, too."

Grace bowed her head, a few strands of blonde hair falling in front of her pixie-like face. "Owen was my boyfriend. Or he pretended to be my boyfriend. Really, he was having an affair with so many other people, and I couldn't bear it any longer, so I did the same to him. I had an affair with Miller."

"And that's why you argued?" I asked, swiveling toward Miller.

My only directive, now, was to stall the pair of them until the detective arrived. If I could do that, well, I could save us. Or the detective could, much to Bee's chagrin.

"Owen and I had a history of trouble," Miller said. "So, yeah, of course, we argued. But things got out of hand when he hurt Grace. She was supposed to be mine. Mine alone, and he decided that he wanted her to be his girl-friend instead." He patted the lobster mallet against his palm. "It was so easy to fool him too. I told him he could bring a date to the restaurant on Monday night for a special time. I expected him to bring Grace. I was going to confront them both, but then he turned up and told me that he'd decided to bring someone else, and I lost my temper."

"Why?" I asked. "What did it matter if he was dating someone else?"

"I told you, Grace is mine. And he was making a fool out of her and a fool out of me by cheating. And that's why Grace has kept quiet all along. She knew what was good for her, and I'm it."

"But..." I trailed off, shaking my head. "But you're in a relationship with Owen's sister."

Grace's jaw dropped. "What? What did you just say?"

This was all so complicated.

Grace had poisoned Owen but hadn't managed to kill him. And then Miller, who was just as much a cheater as the victim himself, had swept in and finished the job. And he'd done it, not out of self-defense or even in a passionate rage, because he wanted to save face. He didn't want to be embarrassed by dating a woman who had been cheated on and made to look like a fool.

Yet, he'd been doing that exact same thing to that exact same woman.

Sheesh. Talk about a soap opera drama. I guess everyone was right. There were loads of people who wanted to kill Owen.

"You're cheating on me?" Grace asked, her face

screwing up. "You're cheating on me?" Tears glistened on her cheeks, but she gritted her teeth instead of breaking down. "How dare you! How dare you do that to me after everything that's happened?"

"Shut up, Grace. You're jumping to conclusions. It's not true. I'm not dating Hannah. Think about it for a second. Everyone in town would have known if I was dating her, and they would have been talking about it."

But Grace wasn't in the listening mood anymore. She let out a terrific yell and launched across the room toward Miller.

He got such a shock he dropped the lobster mallet, and it clunked to the floor. "Grace, relax. It's just a misunder—" The last part of the word was lost to Grace's tackle.

They fell to the floor and rolled back and forth on it, Grace scratching at his face while he tried to hold her back.

"We were supposed to be partners!" Grace shrieked. "You told me that we were partners in crime. In love!"

"That's our cue, I should think," Bee whispered.

We backed away from the scuffling pair. I couldn't look away. It was like watching a Shakespeare-style tragedy unfold in real life. Everyone was having affairs with everyone, a man had been murdered in cold-blooded revenge, and there had been cake. And lobster mallets.

So, less like a Shakespearean tale and more like... a tragedy with lobster mallets. I'd have to look up the literary term for that later.

My back bumped into the door, and I fumbled it open. We struggled out onto the pier just as a cry rang out to the left. Police officers dashed down the boardwalk toward the Lobster Shack, their weapons at the ready. Detective Jones led the pack.

"There we go," I said. "They're in there. They're both involved. Kind of."

But my words were lost on the officers. Detective Jones spared us a brief, thin-lipped glance before disappearing inside to make the arrest.

And that was that.

The mystery was solved. We would no longer be blamed for it. Maybe we'd even get a few intrigued customers at the food truck. I let out a sigh and sat down heavily on one of the pier's many benches, my hands shaking.

"Are you all right?" Bee asked.

"I'm fine," I said, but the panic had finally caught up with me. "I will be fine."

"Good. Because I think we might be here a while. Detective Hobbitfeet will want to talk to us," Bee said.

I threw back my head and laughed. After all, things

could've been worse. We could've been lobster malleted to death or forced to eat fake lobster or any number of horrible outcomes. The mystery was solved. And I could go back to the food truck and do what I'd always wanted to do—serve delicious treats and travel the country.

After we'd fixed up the truck.

Twenty

THE SCENT OF SALT WAS IN THE AIR, THE OCEAN waves rolled and crashed against the beach, and the wind was brisk and chill. Luckily, the sun and the activity had warmed me to the point I barely needed my coat.

I wiped the sweat off my forehead with the back of my hand, then dropped the rag into the bucket of water at my feet with a satisfying plop.

"That's it," I said, spreading my arms. "She's done."

It had only taken us three full days to repair the truck. That included getting the tires replaced, having the windows and windshield repaired, and cleaning everything inside. Now, there was the small feat of restocking, baking, and prepping everything for our first day back on the truck.

"Done?" Bee popped out of the driver's compartment on the truck.

"Done," I announced, grinning at her. "We'll be back in business within a day or two. Hopefully."

"Assuming we don't move on from this town."

Bee came over to stand next to me in front of the truck's open window.

The Oceanside Guesthouse awaited us, its doors open to invite customers and guests inside. Samantha had made it clear that she didn't have another booking for our room and that if we wanted to stay, we were more than welcome to.

"What do you think?" I asked, leaning my hands on the sparkling clean countertop in the truck. "Should we stay another few weeks before we head out? I did tell my supplier to send the boxes to the post office in town."

"Which supplier?" Bee asked.

"For the boxes." I gestured to the collection of striped and branded boxes beneath the counter. "We'll need a fresh supply before we move on to the next town." My idea to be the traveling food truck was ambitious at best and foolhardy at worst, but I'd always preferred ambition over sitting around, waiting for something interesting to happen.

"Stay in Carmel Springs," Bee said, leaning back and

folding her arms. "I don't know if I could handle another week of seeing Detective Jones' frowning face."

"You know, the way you talk about him, I'm starting to think you have a crush on the man."

"You should become a comedian," Bee smirked at me. "No, really, I wouldn't mind staying here. Carmel Springs has a lovely atmosphere. And I'm sure we'll find another restaurant that actually does serve lobster."

My mouth watered at the prospect.

"I have to say, I've enjoyed serving our food on the beach," Bee said. "And in all likelihood, there probably won't be another murder in town."

The crunch of tires on gravel interrupted us. A car had pulled into the parking spot in front of the guesthouse—a black SUV chug-chugging out fumes with black tinted windows. The engine cut off, and both Bee and I fell silent.

The driver's side door clunked open, and a single black dress shoe emerged. It was followed by a man wearing a suit. An exceptionally handsome man with wavy dark hair and matching chocolate-brown eyes. At a guess, I would've placed his age as around thirty years old.

"Hubba hubba," Bee whispered, nudging me. "Looks like Prince Charming has just rolled into town. And he'll be staying at the Oceanside."

"Bee, I would rather eat one of Grace's poison cakes than date another man anytime soon. I've learned my lesson."

"What, that they drop dead the minute you show up for the date?"

"You're too kind."

Bee sniggered. "It was too easy."

"The point is," I whispered, as the man strode around the back of the SUV, ignoring our existence, "that I have no interest in dating any man ever again."

Mr. Handsome opened the passenger side door of the SUV and held out a hand.

"Oh no," Bee said. "Looks like someone beat you to the punch."

A slender woman emerged, her fingers clasping onto Mr. Handsome's for support. She was tall, thin, toned, beautiful, and much younger than him. With swaying platinum blonde hair and the glitzy dress, she could have been a celebrity.

I didn't exactly keep up with social media, so she might've been.

Either way, Blondie stopped and peered around at the parking lot as if it had personally insulted her. She sniffed, raising her nose. "Is this really the best you could do, William?" she asked. "This place?"

"Honey, I told you. This is my hometown. These are my roots."

"Some things are better left in the past."

I agreed with the sentiment, though not the snotty tone in which it was delivered.

"Darling, listen to me," Mr. Handsome said, gripping her hands in his, raising one then the other and delivering a kiss to her fingers. "This is the perfect place for us to get married. You'll see. Eloping was the best idea we ever had."

"No. That you ever had. And it wasn't the best. It was the worst. I don't know how you expect me to plan a wedding on such short notice."

Mr. Handsome—also known as William, apparently— sighed and dropped his fiancée's hands. "It will be great. I'll help you. Or we'll hire a wedding planner. Trust me, this will be a wedding you'll never forget."

She rolled her eyes. "Get the bags, William. I'm going inside for refreshments. Assuming they have running water in a place like this."

She stormed up the steps of the Oceanside and into its waiting reception area.

"Poor Samantha," I whispered. "Can you imagine having to be sweet and hospitable to a woman like that?"

"Jealousy makes you nasty," Bee whispered.

"I'm not—"

William had rounded to the back of the SUV and spotted us. He gave us a confident wave. "Afternoon, ladies. Business going well?"

"Not at all," Bee said.

"But we'll be open tomorrow," I replied. "Hopefully."

"Hopefully," Bee echoed.

"Well, it's nice to know we have some culinary options while we're in Carmel Springs. The last time I was here, they only had one restaurant on the pier, and all it served was lobster, lobster, and more lobster."

"What's wrong with lobster?" Bee muttered to herself.

"That's changed," I said.

"Glad to hear it. I'll see you around." He started unpacking bags from the back. Several of the cases were glittery pink and small. And then there was the massive glassy purple one. The poor man would be out here longer than we would.

"How much do you want to bet she's going to be a nuisance during our stay?" Bee whispered. "The woman. I can see her kicking up a fuss or three."

I turned to Bee, putting the newcomers to the guest-house out of my mind. "So," I said, "what do you say? Want to stay a few more weeks?"

Bee wriggled her lips from side to side. "Hmm. All right. But on one condition."

"Name it," I said.

"No more murders."

I giggled. "Now, Bee, you know I can't promise you that."

Thank you for reading the first of Ruby and Bee's culinary adventures! Marzipan and Murder is available now. Find out what happens at the wedding!

Craving More Cozy Mystery?

If you had fun with Ruby and Bee, you'll, love getting to know Charlie Mission and her butt-kicking grandmother, Georgina. You can read the first chapter of Charlie's story, *The Case of the Waffling Warrants*, below!

"Come in, Big G, come in." I spoke under my breath so that the flesh-colored microphone seated against my throat picked up my voice. "What is your status?"

My grandmother, Georgina—pet name Gamma, code name Big G—was out on a special operation. Reconnaissance at the newest guesthouse in our town, Gossip. The reason? First, she was an ex-spy, as was I, and second, the woman who'd opened the guesthouse was her mortal enemy and in direct competition with my grandmother's establishment, the Gossip Inn.

Who was this enemy, this bringer of potential financial doom?

A middle-aged woman with a penchant for wearing pashminas and annoying anyone who looked her way.

Jessie Belle-Blue.

It was rumored that even thinking the woman's name summoned a murder of crows.

"I repeat, Big G, what is your status?"

"I'm en route to the nest," my grandmother replied in my earpiece.

I let out a relieved sigh and exited my bedroom, heading downstairs to help with the breakfast service.

In the nine months since I had retired as a spy, life in Gossip had been normal. In the Gossip sense of the term. I'd expected that my job as a server, maid, and assistant would bring the usual level of "cat herding" inherent when working at the inn. Whether that involved tracking down runaway cats, literally, or providing a guest with a moist towelette after a fainting spell—tempers ran high in Gossip.

What was the reason for the craziness? Shoot, it had to be something in the water.

I took the main stairs two at a time and found my friend, the inn's chef, paging through her recipe book in the lime green kitchen. Lauren Harris wore her red hair in a French braid today, apron stretched over her pregnant belly.

"Morning," I said, "how are you today?"

"Madder than a fat cat on a diet." She slapped her recipe book closed and turned to me.

Uh oh. Looks like it's time for more cat herding.

"What's wrong?"

"My supplier is out of flour and sugar. Can you believe that?" Lauren huffed, smoothing her hands over her belly while the clock on the wall ticked away. Breakfast was in two hours and Lauren loved baking cupcakes as part of the meal.

"Do you have enough supplies to make cupcakes for this morning?"

"Yes. But just for today," Lauren replied. "The guests are going to love my new waffle cupcakes, and they'll be sore they can't get anymore after this batch is done. Why, I should go down there and wring Billy's neck for doing this to me. He knows I take an order of sugar and flour every week, and I get it at just above cost too. What's Georgina going to say?"

"Don't stress, Lauren," I said. "We'll figure it out."

"Right." She brightened a little. "I nearly forgot you're the one who "fixes" things around here." Lauren winked at me.

She was the only person in the entire town who knew that my grandmother and I had once been spies for the NSIB—the National Security Investigative Bureau. But the news that I had helped solve several murders had spread through town, and now, anybody and everybody with a problem would call me up asking for help. A lot of them offered me money. And I was selective about who I chose to help.

"I'll check it out for you if you'd like," I said. "The flour issue."

"Nah, that's OK. I'm sure Billy will get more stock this week. I'll lean on him until he squeals."

"Sounds like you've been picking up tips from Georgina."

Lauren giggled then returned to her super-secret recipe book—no one but she was allowed to touch it.

"What's on the menu this morning?" I asked.

Lauren was the boss in the kitchen—she told me what to do, and I followed her instructions precisely. If I did anything else, like trying to read the recipe for instance, the food would end up burned, missing ingredients or worse.

The only place I wasn't a "fixer" was in the Gossip Inn's kitchen.

"Bacon and eggs over easy, biscuits and gravy, waffle cupcakes and... oh, I can't make fresh baked bread, can I?"

"Tell her I'll bring some back with me from the

bakery." Gamma's voice startled me. Goodness, I'd forgotten about the earpiece—she could hear everything happening in the kitchen.

"I'll text Georgina and ask her to bring bread from the bakery."

"You're a lifesaver, Charlotte."

We set to work on the breakfast—it was 7:00 a.m. and we needed everything done within two hours—and fell into our easy rhythm of baking and cooking.

My grandmother entered the kitchen at around 8:30 a.m., dressed in a neat silk blouse and a pair of slacks rather than the black outfit she'd left in for her spy mission. Tall, willowy, and with neatly styled gray hair, Gamma had always reminded me of Helen Mirren playing the Queen.

"Good morning, ladies," she said, in her prim, British accent. "I bring bread and tidings."

"What did you find out?" I asked.

"No evidence of the supposed ghost tours," Gamma said.

We'd started hosting ghost tours at the inn recently, so of course Jessie Belle-Blue wanted to do the same. She was all about under-cutting us, but, thankfully, the Gossip Inn had a legacy and over 1,000 positive reviews on Trip-Advisor.

Breakfast time arrived, and the guests filled the quaint dining area with its glossy tables, creaking wooden floors, and egg yolk yellow walls. Chatter and laughter leaked through the swinging kitchen doors with their porthole windows.

"That's my cue," I said, dusting off my apron, and heading out into the dining room.

I picked up a pot of coffee from the sideboard where we kept the drinks station and started my rounds.

Most of the guests had gathered around a center table in the dining room, and bursts of laughter came from the group, accompanied by the occasional shout.

I elbowed my way past a couple of guests—nobody could accuse me of having great people skills—apologizing along the way until I reached the table. The last time something like this had happened, a murder had followed shortly afterward.

Not this time. No way.

"—the last thing she'd ever hear!" The woman seated at the table, drawing the attention, was vaguely familiar. She wore her dark hair in luscious curls, and tossed it as she spoke, looking down her upturned nose at the people around the table.

"What happened then, Mandy?" Another woman asked, her hands clasped together in front of her stomach.

Mandy? Wait a second, isn't this Mandy Gilmore?

Gamma had mentioned her once before—Mandy was

a massive gossip in town. Why wasn't she staying at her house?

"What happened? Well, she ran off with her tail between her legs, of course. She'll soon learn not to cross me. Heaven knows, I always repay my debts."

"What, like a Lannister from *Game of Thrones*?" That had come from a taller woman with ginger curls.

"Shut up, Opal," Mandy replied. "You have no idea what we're talking about, and even if you did, you wouldn't have the intelligence to comprehend it."

The crowd let out various 'oofs' in response to that. The woman next to me clapped her hand over her mouth.

"You're all talk, Gilmore." Opal lifted a hand and yammered it at the other woman. "You act like you're a threat, but we know the truth around here."

"The truth?" Mandy leaned in, pressing her hands flat onto the tabletop, the crystal vase in the center rattling. "And what's that, Opal, darling? I'd love to hear it."

"That you're a failure. You sold your house, left Gossip with your head in the clouds, told everyone you were going to become a successful businesswoman, and now you're back. Back to scrape together the pieces of the life you have left."

"Witch!" Mandy scraped her chair back.

"All right, all right," I said, setting down the coffee pot

on the table. "That's enough, ladies. Everyone head back to their tables before things get out of hand."

Both Opal and Mandy stared daggers at me.

I flashed them both smiles. "We wouldn't want to ruin breakfast, would we? Lauren's prepared waffle cupcakes."

That distracted them. "Waffle cupcakes?" Opal's brow wrinkled. "How's that going to work?"

"Let's talk about it at your table." I grabbed my coffee pot and walked her away from Mandy. The crowd slowly dispersed, people muttering regret at having missed out on a show. The Gossip Inn was popular for its constant conflict.

If the rumors didn't start here then they weren't worth repeating. That was the mantra, anyway.

I seated Opal at her table, and she pursed her lips at me. "You shouldn't have interrupted. That woman needs a piece of my mind."

"We prefer peace of mind at the inn." I put up another of my best smiles.

Compared to what I'd been through in the past— hiding out from my rogue spy ex-husband and eventually helping put him behind bars when he found me—dealing with the guests was a cakewalk.

"What brings you to Gossip, Opal?" I asked.

"I live here," she replied, waspishly. "I'm staying here while they're fumigating my house. Roaches."

"Ah." I struggled not to grimace. Thankfully, my cell phone buzzed in the front pocket of my apron and distracted me. "Coffee?"

"I don't take caffeine." And she said it like I'd offered her an illegal substance too.

"Call me if you need anything." I hurried off before she could make good on that promise, bringing my phone out of my pocket.

I left the coffee pot on the sideboard, moving into the Gossip Inn's spacious foyer, the chandelier overhead off, but catching light in glimmers. The tables lining the hall were filled with trinkets from the days when the inn had been a museum—an eclectic collection of bits and bobs.

"This is Charlotte Smith," I answered the call—I would never get to use my true last name, Mission, again, but it was safer this way.

"Hello, Charlotte." A soft, rasping voice. "I've been trying to get through to you. I'm desperate."

"Who is this?"

"My name is Tina Rogers, and I need your help."

"My help."

"Yes," she said. "I understand that you have a certain set of skills. That you fix people's problems?"

"I do. But it depends on the problem and the price." I didn't have a set fee for helping people, but if it drew me away from the inn for long, I had to charge. I was technically a consultant now. Sort of like a P.I. without the fedora and coffee-stained shirt.

"My mother will handle your fee," Tina said. "I've asked her to text you about it, but I... I don't have long to talk. They're going to pull me off the phone soon."

"Who?"

"The police," she replied. "I'm calling you from the holding cell at the Gossip Police Station. I've been arrested on false charges, and I need you to help me prove my innocence."

"Miss Rogers, it's probably a better idea to invest in a lawyer." But I was tempted. It had been a long time since I'd felt useful.

"No! I'm not going to a lawyer. I'm going to make these idiots pay for ever having arrested me."

I took a breath. "OK. Before I accept your... case, I'll need to know what happened. You'll need to tell me everything." I glanced through the open doorway that led into the dining room. No one looked unhappy about the lack of service yet.

"I can't tell you everything now. I don't have much time."

"So give me the *CliffsNotes*."

"I was arrested for breaking into and vandalizing Josie Carlson's bakery, The Little Cake Shop. Apparently, they found my glove there—it was specially embroidered, you see—but it's not mine because—" The line went dead.

"Hello? Miss Rogers?" I pulled the cellphone away from my ear and frowned at the screen. "Darn."

My interest was piqued. A mystery case about a break-in that involved the local bakery? Which just so happened to be run by one of my least favorite people in Gossip?

And when I'd just started getting bored with the push and pull of everyday life at the inn?

Count me in.

Want to read more? You can grab **the first book** in *the Gossip Cozy Mystery series* on all major retailers.

Happy reading, friend!

Printed in the USA
CPSIA information can be obtained
at www.ICGtesting.com
LVHW042050160724
785670LV00013B/723

9 781776 432301